Pilgrims in the Smoke

Pilgrims in the Smoke

Seven Hebridean Tales

James Shaw Grant

My Word! and Mercat Press
1999

First published in the UK in 1999 jointly by
My Word!, 138 Railway Terrace, Rugby, CV21 3HN and
Mercat Press, 53–59 South Bridge, Edinburgh, EH1 1YS

ISBN 1873644906

Design and typeset by *My Word!*, Rugby, UK

Printed by The Cromwell Press, Trowbridge, UK

In memory of
Callum Macdonald
who gave birth to many poets

Contents

Foreword

In most of these stories I have used the names of real Hebridean villages for places which are fictitious. Some readers may be puzzled, or even annoyed, by the use of a well known name for a village which is quite clearly different geographically and historically from the one the name calls to mind. The practice is not entirely idiosyncratic. I have adopted it to underline the fact that all these stories have one foot at least in the real world. They all began with some fact or incident in my own experience but they have taken off tangentially from that starting point to explore general rather than specific aspects of the truth about the Hebrides. Most of the stories were written twenty years ago and some of them derive from a period much earlier than that. They do not seek to give a contemporary picture of the Hebrides or even a historical retrospect. They try to synthesise my observation of the pressures which bind or break communities, as I have seen them at work, in an experience of a rapidly changing social scene stretching back to the First World War. If I were to give a precise date for the events in any of the stories that would have much the same relation to chronology as my use of real names for imaginary villages.

Pilgrims in the Smoke

PEIGI AND KATE were dissimilar twins. They had only one trait in common. They both invariably wore black.

Peigi was as round as a ball of wool a kitten might play with, or, more accurately, two balls. A large black ball surmounted by the smaller, but still considerable, russet ball of her wind-roughened face. If one judged by her shape and the rubicund face one would expect her to radiate jollity, but everything she said was lugubrious in the extreme.

Kate, on the other hand, was full of fun. With her black clothes falling straight from her slender frame, out of which shot a scrawny neck and an elongated head, she looked, as she said herself, like a lighthouse in mourning. She was a figure by El Greco come alive from the canvas. One could imagine that she had somehow drifted into the Hebrides like the Wandering Jew, and still survived despite the passage of the ages.

"I was born first", she used to say. "They had to pull me out and stretched me in the process. That made things easier for Peigi. She came out the shape the good Lord meant her to be. All my life I've been stretched to make things easier for her."

Having made the statement she would emit a great laugh which seemed to come rumbling from deep down within her, like an earthquake stirring in the bowels of the earth which suddenly rocks the surface with the crunch and fall of solid buildings. She was conscious of the effect her laugh had on strangers, although in her lonely existence she saw few, and apologised quickly with the explanation, "If I didn't use my lungs on Fladdachuain the wind would blow the laugh back down my throat." The explanation would be followed by another earthquake more outrageous than the first.

She did not exaggerate about the wind on Fladdachuain. A pancake of rock and sand in the Atlantic off the coast of the Hebrides, it is surprising it has not been washed out of existence long ago. The breakers, which roar incessantly along the seaward coast, look in winter as if, at any moment, they might sweep the island from side to side. There is neither hill nor herbage to break the continuous Atlantic wind, apart from stunted grasses and little hummocks of sand and bent. The sheep find a sort of shelter in the peaty interior, but even when they lie in the lee of a bank, the wool along the ridge of the spine is ruffled by the wind.

There were half a dozen families on Fladdachuain when Kate married. One by one they left for less arduous conditions on the main island, or went abroad. Her own children left to attend school and university, and were now widely scattered in Canada, Australia and Kenya. Her husband died but she carried on. In winter she was almost completely alone, but in summer there were frequent parties from English schools adventuring in the Hebrides, an occasional artist trying to rediscover the fundamentals of human existence, or, more rarely, a family visit when she would be surrounded for a few weeks by grandchildren, who, to begin with, looked at her suspiciously as a black clothed witch, and retreated in horror from the primitive conditions in which they were expected to live, but who, when they had survived the first cacophonous outburst of affection, which greeted them when they stepped ashore, came to love their granny, as they might a friendly mongrel puppy which licked them unrestrainedly. In later years they looked back on Fladdachuain as a remote paradise where they had once lived through an immeasurably pleasant dream.

Peigi and her husband were among those who moved to the main island. They got their piece of land just across the sound from Fladdachuain, and still used their old croft as summer grazing, ferrying their sheep stock back and fore laboriously in open boats. Although the sisters did not often meet because of the fierce Atlantic swell moving restlessly between them, they communicated on wash days, and when the lamps were lit on winter evenings, at least to the extent that each made a point of watching to see that life on the other side was proceeding normally.

Kate had a small boat she could manage herself, rowing with long sweeps of the oar a man might envy, but the sea was not often calm enough for her to venture out, and when she needed help she flew a flag from a pole at the end of her croft. The flag was generally one of her late husband's shirts, tied to the pole by the sleeves, and Peigi's husband, generally known as the Shark because he was so much at home in the water, would study it carefully through his telescope and draw a conclusion as to the urgency of the call from the particular garment that was flown. Kate's husband had not been richly endowed with shirts, so the choice was restricted, but over the years a convention had grown up between them, although they had never actually discussed it, and the Shark could tell at a glance whether he should go round the coastal villages rousing the ablest of the fishermen for an immediate crossing, irrespective of the danger, or whether he could wait for a day or two for the sea to moderate before setting off with his nearest neighbours.

Peigi generally knew when Kate was coming on her own. She might have claimed, and might even have believed, that it was second sight which made her look out so regularly just at the moment her sister's little craft rounded the point from her own protective bay and began the turbulent crossing. A simpler explanation is that she was schooled to the wind and tide by long experience, although she never handled a boat herself. She never looked out expectantly on the days when it was impossible to cross, but she was always alert in good weather at times when Kate's larder was likely to be low.

She was completely taken by surprise when Kate arrived one day, just after the larder had been replenished. She was even more surprised to see her sister carrying a black sack made out of a discarded skirt. "You're staying the night with us," said Peigi mournfully, as if it were a disaster, although there was nothing she enjoyed more than a visit from Kate.

"It must be forty years since we saw them," was the surprising reply.

"Saw who?" asked Peigi, and the fear stabbed at her heart that Kate had taken leave of her senses. In the instant it took to ask the question, she had visualised all the problems that would arise if she was suddenly required to nurse a sister whose mind was gone but who was robust enough to live for twenty years or more.

"Catriona and Chrissie," said Kate with her great laugh, which despite the fact that she had lived with it all her life, confirmed Peigi in her fears for her sister's sanity. "Whatever put them in your head?" asked Peigi mournfully. "They haven't even bothered to write in the last twenty years." "That's it," said Kate. "We're going to see them."

Peigi looked anxiously at the door to see if there was any sign of the Shark. He liked a blether with Kate and whatever he was doing at the time became much less urgent as soon as she appeared.

"We're going tomorrow," said Kate. "That's why all my clothes are on."

It was then Peigi understood the real source of her worry. Her sister was much plumper than usual, as if she had become bloated overnight by a galloping dropsy. For a fleeting moment Peigi had the illusion that Kate was expanding before her eyes. It was her headgear that gave the clue to the cause. She was wearing all the garments in her wardrobe, one on top of the other, including three hats.

If Kate had stripped off at that moment she could have been used as a textbook on the history, or even the archaeology, of fashion, revealing layer after layer of garments from different dynasties, beginning with a cloche hat, like a Prussian helmet denuded of its spike, which was itself half a century out of date, passing through various phases, each more ancient and more peculiar than the last, until at bedrock, next her thinning hair, the patient investigator would have come on a neatly starched mutch which had graced her grandmother's head when she first became a matron.

Her clothes were even more fantastic. She had three raincoats all of venerable, though widely separated, vintages, and below that an infinite series of blouses, skirts, petticoats, and woolly underwear. Surprisingly, the lower layers would have revealed that, between the sternly black outer garments and the intimate ones which were no one's business but her own, she shone like Joseph's coat of many colours. Black was not the original style of the residents of Fladdachuain, but a garb of mourning, perpetual mourning, which was adopted as the social fabric of the little community crumbled through the loss of the young folk who emigrated, and a morbidly comforting religion came in to fill the vacuum in their elders' emptying lives. But the old gay spirit still persisted beneath the bitter, black veneer.

Peigi looked at the door again, assessing her chance of darting past her crazy sister to seek protection from the Shark, or at least to gain room for manoeuvre on the open croft before the lunatic pounced.

Kate read her look and laughed so vehemently that she rattled the chimes of the old mahogany clock on the mantelpiece. She surveyed herself with the pert and proud, but critically appraising, look of a mannequin.

"It's for the aeroplane," she said, and Peigi's indecision ended.

"Aeroplane!" she cried in dismay and waddled through the door as fast as her fat little legs would take her. Considering her shape, she could have moved more quickly and with much less fuss, if she just lay down and rolled.

If Kate had been philosophically inclined she might have reflected that her sister was not yet acquainted with the principle of the wheel. Instead she sat down in the old rocking chair by the fire and laughed until she cried.

She was still laughing when the Shark put his head round the door, like a mouse reconnoitring, and watched her quietly for several minutes before venturing in.

"What's this about aeroplanes?" he asked at last.

"There was a man in Fladdachuain last summer told me all about them," said Kate. "A poor creature with skinny legs and a pack on his back like a whelk on a crab. Although his legs were skinny, they were that hairy you would hardly believe it. They reminded me of the pony your father had once with the fetlocks shaggier than the tail."

"What business had you with the poor man's legs?" asked the Shark accusingly. Kate's tone had reassured him. Whatever was in the wind was not as sinister as Peigi had imagined, and there was plenty of time for a little fun before they came to the real reason for her visit.

"The poor man hadn't enough trousers to cover them," said Kate. "His trousers stopped at the knee for all the world like a kilt."

"It's just as well he wasn't wearing a kilt if you were all that interested in his legs," said the Shark, and Kate exploded with a mixture of real mirth and simulated anger.

"A man with legs like that would be no use to me," she said. "If you took him by the scruff of the neck he wouldn't be thick enough to make a spirtle for the porridge. As for his legs, you could have used them as knitting needles – if you had fine enough wool."

"He had legs like that and he knew all about aeroplanes," said the Shark with mock amazement.

"It wasn't with his legs he was flying," said Kate by way of explanation. Then she added more seriously, "He told me you can go to Glasgow in less time than it takes me to cross from Fladdachuain."

"Now if you were leaving Glasgow I could see the point of your hurry," said the Shark, "but why on earth does an old woman like you want to go there in the first place?"

"Every night for the last week I've been dreaming of Chrissie and Catriona," said Kate, now completely serious. "I haven't heard from them for twenty years, but I must see them at once and Peigi must come with me."

"Are you sure they want to see you?" asked the Shark.

"They're my own cousins," retorted Kate.

"They were. Twenty years ago," said the Shark. "Are you sure they are today?"

"If they're alive they're my cousins! Yes, and if they're dead!" said Kate, this time with real annoyance. Men could be so stupid. "It's not as simple as that," said the Shark. "On an island like this a man has more cousins than he has in a big city."

"How can that be?" demanded Kate.

"Och," said the Shark. "You lose them in the crowd. They may be there right enough, but you never get near enough to see the earmarks."

"I'll see their earmarks all right," said Kate. "Their ears will be tingling before I'm done with them. All these years and never a line or a whisper, and now they're in and out of my dreams the way they used to be in and out of the house when they were small."

"If you can see them in your dreams that's all right," said the Shark, "but believe me, if you look for them in Glasgow, it's just like an old photo getting spotty with the damp. After all these years what you have in your hand will be less use than a blank sheet of paper."

"Nonsense!" said Kate. "Cousins are cousins. They're not coming into my dreams for nothing and I'm going to find out what they're after."

"Peigi and I will have a wonderful time," she added with a smile. "We've never had a holiday in our lives."

Peigi, who had been listening at the door, crept cautiously in. She and the Shark battled far into the night trying to dissuade Kate from her plan. They were sure it would end in disappointment or worse, but she was not to be moved. "Man, Kate, you're a right barnacle," said the Shark at last, and went to bed. A few days later the two sisters set off in the village bus on the long run to the airport. Peigi was carrying her clothes neatly stowed in a little suitcase she borrowed from the minister's wife. Kate still insisted on wearing every stitch she had, layer upon layer, hat upon hat. She explained to anyone who asked that the man with the skinny legs had told her that they weighed your baggage at the airport and charged you for it. "Even if I was a millionaire," she concluded, "I would grudge paying the man with the aeroplane for carrying my clothes to Glasgow when I can carry them myself, seeing that I'm going anyway."

If she had not been so vigorously persuaded to change her mind, she might have quietly done so, because she was uncomfortably stiff and hot, but the very insistence of her friends that she should listen to reason made it impossible for her to do so.

The airport manager, a lean disgruntled fellow, reacted quickly when he saw the sisters coming through the door. "An urgent phone call," he muttered and disappeared into his private office, leaving his assistant to deal with the apparition.

"Good God!" said the assistant audibly, before he could check himself. Then, under his breath, he added a comment about rats leaving the sinking ship. His boss had a habit of withdrawing suddenly when anything embarrassing seemed likely to arise and this looked like a real crisis.

"It's forty years since I heard from Chrissie and Catriona," said Kate affably, putting her arms on the counter as if preparing for a lengthy chat. "I see," said the assistant, with relief. "They're coming to visit you." If the two old ladies were merely meeting an in-coming flight there was no problem. "They were my mother's brother's children," said Kate, pursuing her own line of thought . "They were twins like ourselves," she added, pointing to Peigi, standing silent in the background with a smile as uncompromising as the day of judgment, although inwardly she was bubbling with excitement at their great adventure.

"They were as like as two peas," Kate continued. "Not like us. They went into service in Glasgow in a big house. They used to tell me that the garden was bigger than the whole of Fladdachuain. There were trees and flowers, and bees in little boxes like hensheds for a puppy. And there was a pond with boats on it, and one day, when the master was away, Chrissie and Catriona took out one of the boats. They thought because they came from Fladdachuain they could row, just like walking, but they had never rowed a boat in their lives before, and they went round and round in circles, laughing and quarrelling, until they lost one of the oars, and the two of them leaned over to catch it, and the boat capsized and they were thrown into the water. They were there all covered with mud and long green weeds in their hair when the master came back and pulled them ashore with a boat hook. It's a good thing the pond wasn't any deeper or I wouldn't be here today. That was the last year they were home in Fladdachuain and they told me the story themselves. They were laughing their heads off as if they had done something clever, but the silly fools might have been drowned. That was in the year of the 'big herring', when the shoals were that thick you could get a fry for dinner by throwing a pail on the end of a rope into the loch from the shore."

"It was a grand life in Fladdachuain in those days," added Kate, who was enjoying herself immensely. "There were lots of young men and women at home. It was just after the Kaiser's war and we were all that poor we couldn't buy a box of matches if we had to, but the fire was never out, and we had food enough, and there were dances and ceilidhs. You wouldn't believe the fun we had dancing eightsome reels in the moonlight on the sands, and the boys would be whirling us round like mad, even when the tide was coming in and the water up to our ankles. One night in a two-step Rory Macusbic, a wild devil, if ever there was one, danced Peigi right into the sea until they were up to their waists, and then he danced her back again, and they went on dancing as if nothing had happened to them, although their clothes were soaking wet and the water was squirting out of their boots. He nearly died of cold after it. His red hair didn't keep him very warm. But Peigi was none the worse. The fat protected her. She's all blubber, like a grey seal."

Kate turned to prod Peigi illustratively, but, without pausing, she went on to tell the frustrated assistant that Rory Macusbic was now working in a grain elevator in Port Arthur, and had a family of three by a girl from Skye, and she was a nice girl in spite of the fact that she was a Sgiathanach, and they had done pretty well for themselves because they came home every other year, but they spent most of their time at the wife's home in Skye, which wasn't very fair to his friends in Fladdachuain, who wanted to see more of Rory and talk to him about the old days. By this time there was a long queue behind the two sisters, and there was quite a lot of coughing, foot shuffling and looking at watches, although those who were nearest to the counter were quite enjoying Kate's reminiscences and the assistant's embarrassment. Several times he attempted to stop the flow, but it was like trying to cork Niagara.

Eventually the sour-faced manager returned, and with a gesture of intense irritation, signalled to the queue to follow him to another desk where he dealt with them himself, while his assistant still battled with the problem of discovering whether Kate and Peigi were meeting an in-coming flight or travelling themselves, and, if they were travelling, whether they were bound for Inverness, Glasgow or London. Or whether, perhaps, they had strayed into the airport by mistake, thinking it was a shop where they could buy a tarasgeir to cut the peats, or perhaps get a setting of eggs to put under a broody hen. He was still trying to puzzle it out when the airport manager announced over the tannoy the departure of the flight to Glasgow.

"That's where we're going," said Kate cheerily, and, taking Peigi by the arm, she followed the crowd aboard the plane, without a ticket or boarding card, but with as much aplomb as if she travelled by plane every day of her life.

When the agitated assistant followed her on board, demanding payment, and then angrily wrote her out a ticket, she smiled at him sweetly, paid him and thanked him, accepting his help as calmly as a queen who takes her seat without looking, because she knows it will be there.

Kate had never had a chair placed for her in her life. Anything she needed she fetched for herself. But long experience had taught her that, when a neighbour got into difficulties, she was helped before she asked. In her innocence she assumed that the whole world was as well ordered as the little community she knew in Fladdachuain.

There was quite a fuss, however, when the air hostess tried to strap her in her seat.

"What do you think I am?" she demanded. "A baby falling out of its pram? Not that I saw many prams in my life, but the minister at Keose had one, and it used to stand outside the manse on a Sunday morning so that all the congregation would be sure to see it. On a Sunday morning, mark you, when any decent baby should be out of sight. But he was an amadan anyway. He might have been all right as a schoolmaster or a janitor, but in the pulpit he was as much use as a cockerel shouting to all the world what he has done."

There was no opportunity for explanations under the torrent of Kate's eloquence, but she was so intent on telling the story of the Keose minister's pram, that the air hostess was able to strap her in before she realised what was happening. The air hostess no sooner moved away, however, than Kate began struggling to extricate herself. She had spotted an old acquaintance at the other end of the plane, and saw no reason why she should not pay her a visit.

By this time the plane had begun to taxi and a terrified air hostess pushed Kate back into her seat by main force, and held her there with a hand on her chest, until the plane was safely airborne. Just as the warning light went off, Kate brushed her aside and lumbered down the aisle. She borrowed brief cases, as she went, from astonished business men, and used them, as she would have used peats, to make a stool beside her friend.

Peigi meantime sat with her hands clasped tightly in her lap, praying fervently for the safety of her own fireside. She watched in disbelief as the sheep, the cows, the houses, the fishing boats, the sea, and finally the clouds themselves fell away beneath her feet, as they passed through a Hebridean rainstorm to the clear air above. When the plane suddenly filled with sunshine, Peigi looked up in terror, as if she expected to see an angel peering through the window or maybe even God himself.

Although Kate was blocking the aisle, the staff decided to take no action until they were ready to commence the descent into Glasgow. At that point the air hostess took her gently by the arm and explained, "You must go back to your seat now and strap yourself in for landing." "Back to the pram!" said Kate, in great good humour, and her laugh rang through the plane terrifying even the most seasoned passengers.

"Yes," said the hostess, humouring the eccentric. "Back to the pram. We cannot land until baby is sitting down properly and well strapped in."

"Just tell the driver to hold on a minute," said Kate affably, "until I finish the story I'm telling Annie the Bullock. You know Annie? Surely! Everyone knows Annie."

"Hurry," said the hostess as she heard the landing wheels snap into place. "We cannot get down until you are in your seat." "And what's wrong with staying up?" asked Kate. "I'm enjoying myself and it's not often I have the chance of a yarn with Annie. Do you know why we call her the bullock?"

"This is worse than a bloody hi-jack," whispered the co-pilot as he came to the assistance of the air hostess. Between them they frog-marched Kate back to her seat. She accepted the treatment with great good humour as evidence of the eccentricity of the Sasunnach, who are too impatient and too ill-mannered to wait for the end of a conversation between friends.

"That's the best ceilidh I had in years," she said to Peigi as she was dumped in the seat beside her. Peigi was too petrified to reply as she saw the great size of Glasgow, and the tenements racing up to meet her.

When the plane door was opened, two burly policemen stepped in and waved the impatient passengers back to their seats. "Where are they?" they asked, and the co-pilot pointed to Kate and Peigi.

The security guards in the Hebrides had watched with amazement as Kate, bulging all over and wearing a pyramid of hats, had sailed majestically past them, refusing to be searched. An altercation ensued between them and the airport staff. They wanted Kate and Peigi off the plane to go through the routine. The airport staff said they were harmless lunatics and the sooner they got rid of them the better. The security men were inwardly convinced, but asserted their authority by pretending otherwise and alerting the police.

Before the first policeman to reach her could speak, Kate threw her arms in the air and shattered the plane with another laugh. "Tarmod Billy," she exclaimed. "I never saw you in my life before, but I would know you on your father supposing I met you in the moon."

"I'm not with you, hen," said the surprised policeman in a Glasgow accent which startled Kate.

"That's a terrible way to speak for a man from Fladdachuain," she said.

"Come along, hen," said the policeman taking her arm. "I don't know what you're on about. I've never heard of Fladdachuain."

There followed the most astonishing cross-examination a Glasgow policeman has ever been subjected to. There was nothing he could do to stop the torrent of questions which Kate directed at him, and they were so natural, uninhibited, and insistent, and delivered with such calm authority, he answered them meekly, against both his judgment and his will.

Eventually Kate was satisfied that, although the policeman was not the man she thought, he was in fact a third cousin, although the poor fellow had never been to Fladdachuain and couldn't speak Gaelic.

"What did I tell you?" she said triumphantly to Peigi. Then turning back to the policeman she said to him sweetly, "You can't mistake the Tarmod Billies anywhere. They're for all the world like the bull we had from the Department with a white spot on it's backside, and before we got rid of it every calf in the island had a spot in the self-same place. It's funny how some families have a mark like that you cannot rub off."

By this time she was satisfied the policeman was an old friend who would see her safely on the next stage of her journey, and she went with him jauntily, until she realised she was being handed over to two hard-faced policewomen, who had instructions to strip her to the buff, and give her belongings a thorough going over. The policewomen had not got very far before they realised they had more on their hands than they could cope with. Kate would not be persuaded, and all the policewomen in Glasgow could not have held her still for long enough to strip the onion skin by skin.

"It's an anaesthetic she needs," said one of the exasperated officers in a moment of blind inspiration. "Are you a doctor?" asked Kate, instantly docile.

"The doctor's assistant," replied the quick witted policewoman.

"That's different," said Kate, and the clothes began to tumble from her in cascades. She knew about medical examinations for intending emigrants, and saw little difference between going to Glasgow and going to Detroit. They were equally remote from Fladdachuain.

The policewomen watched with amazement as the coats, the blouses, the jumpers, the skirts, the petticoats, and multifarious under garments, were heaped on the floor, while the burly woman, they had been afraid to grapple with, shrank before them until she looked like a knobbly clothes pole.

In the meantime, Tarmod Billy's third cousin, if such in fact he was, searched Kate's black bag with even greater astonishment. What felt to the touch like sticks of gelignite emerged as black puddings. The hand grenades were eggs carefully wrapped in so many layers of newspaper they were thrice the normal size. One of the policewomen came out to report their suspect clean just as the groping hand emerged with a fish head stuffed with a sort of dry porridge."Cean cropic," said the second policeman, who was in fact an islander, although he concealed the fact so that he could continue to enjoy Kate's running commentary in Gaelic, as she told Peigi what she thought of the people around her, and their fathers and their fathers' fathers. His explanation was drowned by the scream of the policewoman as she saw the glassy eyes of the haddock staring at her from the policeman's hand, and the even louder scream which followed from the policeman himself as he put in his hand and took out the final exhibit.

By this time he was pretty well convinced that Kate was merely odd, but he still had a lingering doubt. Her oddness, and all the domestic items in the bundle, might be an extremely clever cover up for the hard, unidentified object right at the bottom of the bag which was carefully packed in what felt like damp sawdust. He took the parcel out carefully and opened it. Very gingerly he began to clear the sawdust off to see what it was protecting. He had just caught a glimpse of the black metallic colour of his find when the lobster snapped and all but severed his thumb.

Kate had by this time emerged from the cubicle to see what all the screaming was about. She was still only half-dressed, although very adequately covered, but as she was at the multi-coloured stage, not having reached the obligatory outer black, the policeman was almost as surprised as if she had come out in the nude.

"It's for Chrissie," said Kate, indicating the lobster. "She was always fond of them, but Catriona can't stomach them at all. Catriona'll take the puddings."

"Have you a car?" she asked the policeman.

"We have a Panda," he replied, still unable to resist her questions, although he cursed himself for being a softy.

"Does it go on wheels like a Ford?" asked Kate.

"It is a Ford," said the policeman.

"Why then do you call it a Panda?" asked Kate.

Foolishly the policeman began to explain the functions of a Panda, but, when he became bogged down in the operations of the city police, Kate rescued him with a brusque interruption. "Have you got it with you?" "It's outside," said the policeman.

"That's fine," said Kate. "You'll take me to Chrissie's. The sooner she has that lobster the better. The puddings will keep."

"What's her address?" asked the policeman, who at last saw a chance to get rid of his incubus.

"There it is," said Kate, handing him a grubby slip of paper torn from the top of a letter.

"Hell!" said the policeman. "She's not living there."

"Why not?" demanded Kate.

"There's nothing there but a hole in the ground."

"That's her address," said Kate doggedly.

The policeman looked carefully at the slip of paper. "When on earth did you get this?" he asked.

"I'm not sure, was it 1925 or 1926?" said Kate. "It was a good summer anyway."

Tarmod Billy's cousin groaned. "If you can't take us there, maybe you can put us up for the night," said Kate. "I'm bound to see her if I go through the village in the morning. She'll be around the croft. It's too early for the peats."

"You're stuck with her," said the Gaelic-speaking policeman, who had kept discreetly in the background. "You'll have to find Chrissie or share your bed with the long one." In the end, all the city's resources for the detection of crime were mobilised to find two women named Chrissie and Catriona, who were last heard of forty years ago, living in a street which had been demolished in the blitz, who were both believed to have married, but whose husband's names, occupations and whereabouts were completely unknown.

Kate poured out volumes of information about their antecedents in Fladdachuain. She even provided the address of their relatives in Kalamazoo. But she had no information of any sort that would help to establish their whereabouts in Glasgow. Unlike most Highland folk in the city, they had severed all connection with their island roots. Tarmod Billy's cousin was appalled at the waste of time. His silent companion took over, and quickly found the answer.

A few words in Gaelic on the Panda's radio, explaining the situation in graphic terms, sent a wave of mirth around the city, mingled with the sullen curiosity of the uninitiated, who listened to the conversations which ensued, glum and hostile. Those within the freemasonry of the Gael had their laugh, and then responded with a fund of information. Catriona was quickly identified, but there was some doubt whether Chrissie was still alive.

When the Gaelic-speaking policeman returned from the Panda with

Catriona's address, Tarmod Billy's cousin whistled long and loud. "God Almighty," he said. "Someone's in for a hell of a shock." Kate paid no attention to the comment. She was annoyed she could not go direct to Chrissie with the more perishable of her gifts.

"It's just like Chrissie," she said. "She's never around when you want her. Even when you're bringing her a lobster. She used to wander off by herself for hours along the shore and she didn't want anyone with her. They used to say she was writing poems in her head, but I don't think she was as daft as that."

"Come along hen," said the policeman edging her towards the Panda.

"You too," said his companion in Gaelic, giving a more vigorous nudge to Peigi. Throughout the proceedings she had been, not silent, but rather like the drone of the bagpipes, maintaining a continuous dribble of querulous noise which would be monotonous to the point of insanity by itself, but is almost unnoticed as background to the real tune.

Over and over again, in the same unvarying voice, she lamented the shame that had come upon her. "The suitcase I got from the minister's wife, emptied by strangers! It's on me the two days came, when I'm stripped to the skin in the middle of Glasgow, and women in blue clothes and men's bonnets go through my petticoat looking for fleas."

In the Panda Kate was silent, watching the traffic with interest and incredulity. Peigi, unseeing, kept up her lament, which became more and more irritating, until it stopped abruptly in an access of fear as the Panda swept between two immense pillars, carrying wrought iron gates in a high wall, and pulled up before the biggest building she had ever seen. Bigger even than Torosay Castle where the Shark had worked occasionally as a river watcher, when he was not himself engaged in poaching the Sasunnach's salmon.

"Is this a prison?" she asked in dismay.

Kate gave a great laugh. "No," she said. "This is where your cousin Catriona is a skivvy now."

"Hardly a skivvy," said the policeman, gently. "She's the boss. This is a business college, and she's the head."

The policeman thought it advisable to accompany them and smooth the way. There was a somewhat embarrassed smile on his face when, a few minutes later, he ushered the sisters into the Principal's room, Kate still bloated by her multiplicity of garments, still surmounted by the three hats which added to her already incongruous height.

It was a large room, opulent and bristling with efficiency. The walls were lined with bookcases and filing cabinets. The large desk was deep in in-trays and out-trays, reference books, files and telephones. But there was no suggestion of clutter. Everything was marshalled precisely on its proper toe mark, like guardsmen at a Royal review.

Behind the desk sat a formidable, square-built woman, with only the vaguest resemblance to the skinny little girl Kate had known in Fladdachuain.

It was as if Catriona had ceased to be herself and had become a relative by a collateral line in which had mingled the blood of barrel-chested warriors. Strong men quailed in her presence, but Kate was unabashed. She marched across to the desk, still carrying in her hand, as if it were the most natural thing in the world, the black puddings, from which she removed the wrapping as she went, so that Catriona could savour immediately the treat which had meant so much to her as a child. "I made them myself, just the way you like them," she said breezily.

"Who are you?" demanded Catriona, eyeing the puddings with distaste.

"Your cousin Kate."

"Did I ask you to call?"

"No. I just came."

"Have you an appointment?"

"We don't use them in Fladdachuain." said Kate, settling into a chair. "What are your ones like?" She winked at Peigi to signal that she had carefully chosen a form of reply which would establish what an appointment was without revealing that she did not already know. Peigi missed the point, but Catriona didn't, and moved in ruthlessly.

"You wouldn't know," she said. "You don't organise your time in Fladdachuain. You don't even use it. You squander it."

"It passes very pleasantly anyway," said Kate giving no indication that she had detected the contempt in Catriona's voice.

"See here," said Catriona, showing Kate her large desk diary. "Every working hour of every day is divided up and allocated before the day begins. Not a moment is unaccounted for or wasted. I have no time for casual callers or idle chatter. I have things to do. Important things." She closed the book with a dismissive slam. "Peigi thought this was a prison," said Kate with her great laugh. "She thought the polis was going to lock us up. It never crossed her mind that you were one of the prisoners." She pointed at the desk diary. "That's worse than gutting herring at the Yarmouth fishing. At least there were days when the fleet was blank and you had nothing to do but walk the streets, and knit, and sing, and tease the coopers. It was great fun work in those days when you hadn't any to do."

Before Catriona could intervene again, she planted the black puddings on the desk. "I brought these for your tea, and I wish you would fry them right away. I'm famished. I haven't had a bite to eat since leaving Fladdachuain."

With an ill grace Catriona buzzed her secretary and ordered tea. It seemed the only way to get rid of her visitors. The time until the tea came was taken up by Kate's confused chatter of island and family gossip, which angered Catriona by its irrelevance to anything she was interested in. She was even more angered by Kate's insistence that Catriona had come to her repeatedly in her dreams, asking for help.

"I certainly don't need your help," said Catriona surveying the apparition. "Or anyone else's."

"Why then did you come to me?" demanded Kate.

"I'm not responsible for your hallucinations," said Catriona.

"I don't know what that means," said Kate. "But I know what it means when my own cousin comes crying for help after not writing me for forty years."

Before Catriona could reply, the tea arrived and Kate exploded. She looked at the tiny individual cups, without the back-up of a teapot, and the skimpy plate of pallid weight-reducing biscuits.

"A house like a castle and a tea that would starve a mouse!"

When Catriona had shown her contempt for Fladdachuain's time-wasting habits, it was a civilised contempt, icy but restrained. A stiletto slipped between the ribs. Dislike veneered with a smile. Kate's contempt was uninhibited. It reverberated through the room like the foghorn on the lighthouse she compared herself with.

"Can you not put on the griddle and make a decent scone?" she demanded.

"I didn't ask you to come," said Catriona. "I have no wish to know you or listen to your gossip. I turned my back on Fladdachuain as soon as I realised what a purposeless, dead end, claustrophobic life you lead there, with nothing to do but picking each other's nits. Fladdachuain is a backwater. Flotsam left by the passing tide. I'm swimming now in an open sea. I have a rich, free, productive life, and a real sense of achievement."

"We'll go to Chrissie," said Kate decisively. "This one is mad." Hurt and puzzled, she realised that Catriona had rejected her. The loss was Catriona's, but there was nothing she could do about it, meantime anyway. Catriona, she felt, was an aberration, but there could hardly be two in the same family.

"Where does Chrissie live?" she demanded.

Catriona hesitated. Kate had put her finger on a sensitive spot. Then with a brusqueness which was the blood brother of Kate's, although it seemed cold and hard and impersonal, while Kate's was the blundering intrusion of a friendly inquisitive animal, she opened a filing cabinet and took out a folder.

"That's the last news I had of Chrissie," she said, placing the folder in front of Kate with a movement as decisive as a bite.

"Her own sister in a brown envelope like a catalogue from the postman," said Kate in amazement. She thumbed the contents of the file without understanding them. Without really seeing them. It was not the way she was accustomed to get news of her relations.

The policeman stepped across and lifted the top sheet. He had recognised it as a Sheriff Court summons.

"Chrissie is in trouble," he said gently. He knew now who Chrissie was. "She's a wino," he added.

"What's that?" asked Kate.

He explained as tactfully as he could, expecting that it would come to Kate as a shock. Instead she let out a great disbelieving bellow. She knew that men were sometimes addicted to drink. There had been very little of it in Fladdachuain in recent years, in fact there had been little social life of any sort, but in her younger days she had seen men drunk and thought them funny. It was one of the endearing aberrations of the human male that he never ceased to need mothering. A woman addicted to drink was, however, quite beyond the bounds of credibility.

"She appeared before me in the Court," said Catriona. "She had married a second time after I lost trace of her. She may have married a third time too for all I know. Anyway the name meant nothing to me when I saw it on the charge sheet. Then they took her in and put her in the dock. It was difficult enough to recognise her even then. Of course I could not take the case myself and I had to tell them why. I never felt so ashamed in all of my life." "And how did Chrissie feel?" asked Kate, pointedly. She now realised that it was all true, and Chrissie's life style was just as remote as Catriona's from anything known on Fladdachuain.

"Chrissie is beyond feeling," said Catriona dismissively. "Certainly I'm beyond any feeling for her. She had the same start in life as I had. God knows the time and money I spent on her when I saw that she was going adrift. But she was determined to go her own way."

"Do you know where she stays?" Kate asked the policeman.

"It's on the charge sheet, but I wouldn't advise you to see her," he replied.

"I have a lobster for her," said Kate.

"She won't thank you for a lobster," said the policeman. "The only thing she would thank you for is the last thing she should have."

"Never mind the riddles," said Kate. "At least she'll give me a bed for the night."

"Chrissie hasn't seen a bed for many years," said the policeman. "It will do neither you nor her any good to meddle. Just leave her to us."

"She's not your cousin," said Kate decisively, picking up her bundle and stalking from the room. When the policeman overtook her, she was already in the Panda. "You just take me there," she commanded.

Peigi had sat silent during the whole visit, but before waddling out after Kate and the policeman, she apologised to Catriona by whom she was much impressed. "You know Kate," she said. "What is in comes out, like a man vomiting. But she doesn't mean any harm."

Catriona was strangely subdued that evening as she told her husband of the day's events. He was a surgeon, quiet, competent, unassertive, with the gentleness almost of a woman, although underneath he was tougher than Catriona herself. Her brittle show of domineering efficiency covered a great deal of uncertainty and self-questioning.

"You've seen a ghost," he said when she had finished her selective and somewhat defensively coloured account of her brush with Kate.

"There are no ghosts," she said scornfully. "I don't mean a ghostly ghost. I mean a real one," he said. "You have seen yourself as you might have been if you had fallen on the Fladdachuain side of the fence, instead of mine."

"It was luckier for me than for you it worked out that way," he added hastily as he realised how smugly offensive his comment had been.

"I had broken loose from Fladdachuain before I ever met you," she replied with some acerbity. "I made my escape deliberately and anyone with the requisite ability could have done the same. I came away because I did not belong to Fladdachuain. Kate stayed because she did."

"If it's as simple as that, what's worrying you?" asked Jack.

"What right has a lunatic with three hats got accusing me of callousness?" said Catriona angrily.

"Did she?" asked Jack. "You hadn't said."

"She didn't directly," said Catriona, "but why else did she come?"

"She didn't know the circumstances when she came," said Jack. "She's not accusing you. You're accusing yourself. What are you going to do about it?"

"Do?" she exclaimed.

"You can't leave things as they are," he said.

"I can," she replied. "And I will."

It was at that moment Kate and Peigi arrived with the ambulance. In the interval they had made an excursion in the Panda, which Kate always referred to afterwards as "the day we went to hell with a Glasgow polis."

She was familiar with poverty: throughout her life she was seldom far removed from it. She was also familiar with dirt. As a child she shared a roof with the cattle and the hens. Even now her boots and her hands were never clean for long, as she ploughtered round the croft in mud and manure. These were physical facts which were unavoidable. They affected the husk but not the kernel. You improved the conditions, if you could, but even if you could not escape, you did not succumb.

What she had not seen before was the decay of substantial buildings into windowless, doorless, stairless, rat infested, squalid hovels, and their acceptance as a refuge by those who had lost the will, or lacked the ability, to resist their own decline as human beings. She had once seen a cow sink into a bog and perish, despite the efforts of the men from two townships with planks and ropes. But that was a natural disaster, and the whole resources of the family, and their neighbours, had been spent in trying to avert it. Here, although she did not put the thought into philosophic terms, or into words of any sort, although she sensed it with every nerve, the bog itself was a human artefact. There was no visible effort to save the victims, and they were in the bog, it would appear, not entirely by chance. She had the feeling, right or wrong, that they had sought it out and were wallowing in it with a strange despairing contentment.

The policeman took them down a dismal street where their feet crunched on broken glass, some of it from the vanished windows, but more from bottles smashed against the wall in frenzy and disgust when the last precious life-destroying drop was gone.

The down pipes stopped a good six feet or more from the worn, fragmented sidewalk, and, from the severed shanks, water poured in sombre cataracts. The sound conjured up for Kate a picture of the hills she looked on across the strait from Fladdachuain, where thin threadlike waterfalls danced and tinkled in every gully, except in rare periods of drought. The contrast heightened her sense of human dereliction all around her.

Flashing his torch, the policeman led her through a close into a backyard where the feel of the mud clinging to her boots, although she could not see it, again reminded her of home and the contrast. She looked in terror at the great, gaunt, windowless walls rearing over her, as if they would collapse at any moment, and the furnace glow of the sodium lights of the city reflected from a sodden sky. She felt that she had penetrated to the bottomless pit she had read of in the Bible, while the fires of hell burnt silently so far above her head that even the cries of the damned were muted.

From the back green the policeman led the way into one of the houses, if house it could still be called. The windows were gone, and although a door of sorts still hung limply from the hinges, it was half eaten away as if gnawed by mammoth rats, where the inmates had hacked with any tool they could find in a frantic search for firewood. In a corner of the room, beneath a pile of filthy sacking, Chrissie lay dying with an empty bottle by her side.

The policeman felt the flickering pulse. "Get an ambulance, quick," he said, signalling to his mate to return to the Panda to make the call. "I don't think they can do anything for her," he said to Kate. "But we'll get her to hospital as quickly as we can."

"She's not going to any hospital," said Kate decisively. "She'll die in clean sheets in her sister's home."

"They took her here without my authority, and they can just take her away again," said Catriona, when the arrival of the ambulance was announced.

"That's all right for you," said her husband quietly. "but I happen to be a doctor."

"The hypocritic oath!" said Catriona with a sneering malice which startled him.

She had never spoken to him like that before, but he realised that, although it was directed at him and wounded him, it was not meant personally. It was the random flailing of a normally composed individual who had been deeply hurt herself, and was struggling to contain a whirling vortex of intimate, personal memories, charged with hatred, pity, guilt, compassion, pride and naked terror, set suddenly in motion by those incongruous apparitions from the past: her sister – her twin – dying in a drunken stupor and her ludicrous cousin with the clownish hats, stalking unbidden into her life, tearing down the defences she had struggled so hard to erect.

"The students are on holiday, so the dormitories are empty," said Jack. "I'll get a nurse we can trust to be discreet." As he spoke he went to the door to give the necessary instructions to the ambulancemen. Then crossed to the telephone to arrange for a nurse.

"Your cousins can sleep in the same room as the patient. They can be sure that everything possible is done for her, but I'll see that the nurse keeps firm control," said Jack. Catriona made no reply.

When Jack returned some hours later she was still sitting by the fire without even the pretence of reading. It was the first time he had seen her completely idle in all the years he had known her.

"Chrissie may last until morning, but she certainly won't last another night," he said.

Catriona looked up anxiously, but he anticipated her fear.

"The funeral will be in Fladdachuain," he said. "I'll get a charter plane. Your cousins want to take her home with them, –and I rather like the idea. At least it will be peaceful in Fladdachuain, and God knows she's due a little peace."

"What went wrong, Jack? Was it anything I did or didn't do?" she asked with an uncertainty and a humility which were equally foreign to her.

"You were always good at organising other people's lives, but you're not quite God," he replied, trying to raise a laugh. "You have no need to blame yourself for causing it, or even for not preventing it. But now that it's happened, we can't wash our hands of it."

Three days later, Catriona was back in Fladdachuain for the first time in forty years. She offended against local custom by following the coffin to the grave and standing by while the menfolk lowered it reverently into the sand, but no one criticised her for the breach. They read it as evidence of the deep love she bore her sister, and quite understood that, after forty years, she might easily have forgotten how these things were conducted in Fladdachuain.

The Sheriff's Dry Shebeen

THE MOST SOPHISTICATED Court Room in Europe existed for a number of years in the little town of Carbost in the Western Isles. Judges, lawyers and sociologists came from all over the world to see it and marvel.

The special qualities of the Court Room derived from the Gaelic revival in the dying years of the twentieth century, when it was decided that the civil rights of Hebrideans demanded that they should have their legal business, civil or criminal, conducted in the language of their choice. Gaelic or English as the pursuer (or accused) preferred.

The man who achieved fame, or notoriety, through devising the Court Room, was a dry, unimaginative civil servant whose name has a strange, irrelevant resonance Sir Thomas Abeckett. The country's leading authority on constitutional law, he was utterly opposed to the whole idea of giving Gaelic legal status although, oddly, it was he who made it possible.

He was in Carbost for a fishing holiday when the Government announced its new policy. He loved the islands. Scenically, that is, as a backdrop to his own private thoughts. Islanders and their language were quite another matter. What should have been a tranquil, relaxing holiday became a torment. He knew there was only one question in life worth asking, in his situation: would the salmon rise? But he could not focus his attention in any pleasurable way on the business in hand when he made his cast. In the past, when he overheard the ghillies whispering together in Gaelic, he imagined they were exchanging the current gossip of their provincial little town. He amused himself, for hours, as he laboured pleasantly with the rod, trying to imagine what petty scandal among their crofter neighbours was engaging their attention so completely. Now he saw things differently. They were not gossips. They were conspirators: anarchists! plotting the overthrow of the constitution. Thank God the overarching power had been reserved to Westminster!

His nightmare ended when he passed through Carbost on his way to the Airport, at the end of his holiday. In the past he had been amused at the row of Pakistani shops in the centre of the town. It didn't say much for the enterprise of the natives that a group of itinerant packmen as they were when they first arrived had penetrated so far into the Highland wilderness and prospered so greatly. This time, however, he saw the Pakistani enclave with a new insight and a sudden illumination.

If Parliament granted the natives, who were all now bilingual and thoroughly proficient in English, the right to have their legal business transacted in Gaelic, would not the refusal of similar facilities, in Urdu, to Pakistani Hebrideans, constitute racial discrimination? Are the rights of a minority within a minority less than the rights of a minority within a majority? It was the sort of question he could chew over for ever, although he quite missed the point that only a small percentage of Pakistanis speak Urdu, although it is one of their two official languages, and the even more important point that the other official Pakistani language is English.

Soon his logical, searching mind, took him even further. Carbost was a harbour of refuge for vessels flying a multitide of flags. Most significantly it was resorted to by fishing vessels from other European countries. The skippers and owners were frequently in trouble for breaking the complicated quota laws imposed unavailingly to prevent over fishing. Had they not the same right as British citizens to be tried in the language of their choice, for any offences they were alleged to have committed. Wasn't that what Europe was all about?

Everyone assumed that Sir Thomas used the Pakistani gambit, as it came to be called, solely to defeat the Gaelic claim for equal status and many Lowland Scots hoped in private he would win the day, although they did not say so publicly, in case their party lost the Highland vote. The assumption, was right when the argument began but, by the end, he was working to quite another agenda. Although it was not then generally known, his nephew had invented a method of instantaneous translation by computer, without the intervention of interpreters. The apparatus was very costly but very efficient. A witness could reply to a question in his mother tongue but a dozen, a score, of people could hear him immediately in whatever language they chose, from their own console. It was dramatic. It was Biblical. But was it Babel or Pentecost that had come again?

The philosophic, the constitutional, the political issues were quickly forgotten. Here was money! A British patent which every Court Room in the world would need, once it was installed in one!

The Government showed considerable imagination in making the first installation in the heart of the Gaeltachd and in a busy fishing port. It enabled them to claim, within the Highlands, that they were raising the status of Gaelic in support of the local people and to claim, outside the Highlands, that they were merely complying with their commitments to the European Union, without any special concession to the teuchtars. The Government also realised that such a high tech installation in a tiny country Court would attract even more attention throughout the world than a similar installation in the main court of a national capital.

The international sales of the British equipment would be immense.

Sir Thomas had never been popular in the island where he came to fish. He was an incomer, an alien, trying to deny the islanders their God given right to poach. Now he became something of a hero. Almost a saint. He had conferred on the Island's petty offenders the inestimable privilege of being fined or imprisoned in Gaelic rather than in English. A privilege which, not surprisingly, was appreciated more by the island's politicians than by those who went to gaol.

There was, however, a good deal more to it than that. For local councillors life became one long Hogmanay as they entertained delegations from governments around the world, hurrying to the Hebrides to see the miracle at work. The interest was greatest where the language problem was most acute. Africans and Polynesians, from little enclaves one had never heard of, became familiar figures wandering, at times a little disconsolately, through the Island rain.

The Tourist Board advertised the Sheriff Court as one of the island's main attractions. More important even than the local museums and archaelogical remains. It was a hands on experience. That was the great appeal. Everyone who attended court had to have his own console to listen to the evidence, in the language he understood. The visitor could play the console like an organ, ignoring the meaning of what was said but listening to the sound of the words in an ever changing medley of languages as if it was a new form of music, just arrived from outer space.

The Board even went so far as to manufacture litigation so that the Court was busy in the summer season when there were visitors around. They drew the line at fomenting crime but it was easy to rustle up cases in the Land Court. Arguments about boundaries. Disputes about peat banks. Family quarrels about succession which involved the court in abstruse matters of genealogy, made all the more perplexing by the fact that there were so many people sharing so few surnames and sometimes a Christian name as well. One dispute concerned a father and three sons, all called John Mackenzie, according to their birth certificates. The crofters knew what was going on and joined in the fun. They conducted their own pleadings without solicitors and were quite happy to hype up a non existent dispute in a good cause. It was a new form of amateur drama, involving whole villages, in which the actors and actresses made up the lines as they went along. While the summer was occupied presenting their "plays", the winter evenings were pleasantly employed in making up the next year's programme.

Some of the island reporters also spotted the commercial possibilities. Instead of trying to squeeze a few shillings lineage out of a trivial case, by giving it a twist which, in truth, it never had, they now recorded cases verbatim, in a mixture of languages, and took orders from visitors to the Court for tapes of the cases they had heard. These mixtures of meaningless sound soon outsold the island's most famous songs.

The most successful enterpreneur was the Bar Officer of the Court, known locally as the Monk. The nickname had no ecclesiastical significance. It was an abbreviation of Monkey, a name conferred on him when he was courting.

A tiny man, as quick and lithe as an eel, he had a rival who looked down on him and sneered from six foot four. One evening, by mischance, the two of them arrived together at the lady's home. The rival, smiling at the girl friend, placed the palm of his hand flat against the ceiling. "Can you do that?" he asked with a dismissive gesture, The little fellow turned a somesault on to the kitchen table and placed the soles of his feet against the ceiling. "Can you do that?" he replied, still upside down and standing on his hands.. In that moment he became, simultaneously, the victor in love and the Monkey.

The Monk, because of his duties, had the keys to the Court House. Surreptitiously, at night, he admitted visitors, for a substantial fee. Behind the shuttered windows, he let them play with the equipment to their heart's content. Instead of snapshots or a video, they took home from their holiday a tape of themselves, chatting together in all the languages of Europe or indeed the world as if they knew them all. Few of them suspected that the state of mutual incomprehension the resulting tape portrayed was a metaphor of most communications within their marriages, even when both partners used the same dialect of the same mother tongue. Misapprehension of what other people say is the normal human condition, even, perhaps especially, in the home.

The Monk's moonlighting was well known in Carbost. It was popularly referred to as The Sheriff's Dry Shebeen, because the Sheriff was the one person in town who did not know of its existence. Once, he almost stumbled on it. He left some urgent private papers in his chambers and went back at night to get them. The Dry Shebeen was going merrily as he approached but the Monk, who had been a naval reservist, had a look out posted. By the time the Sheriff climbed the stairs, the Court House was dark and orderly and completely empty. If the Sheriff had run his finger over some of the sophisticated apparatus, of which he was so proud, he might have detected a little residual heat, indicating recent use. If he had wandered into the cells, he would have been even more surprised. Every hue of human flesh was packed into the tiny cubicles, a little indiscrimenately, in the hurry. The dark, the silence, and the close proximity produced the inevitable result. His Lordship would have been shocked, as an elder of the Kirk, but, as a lawyer, he would have realised that consenting adults are consenting adults even in a prison cell.

Needless to say, the excitement of the raid and all that followed made that evening the highlight of the holiday for those involved. They had their tapes to give their tale credibility while the confused emotions, aroused by whatever happened in the cells, produced new drama every time they told it. Some boasted! Some invented! Some denied! Some accused! But always, when they told the tale, the partners quarrelled. The orgy in the Sheriff's Dry Shebeen went echoing round the world in laughter and recrimination. In new romances and exceedingly bitter divorces.

The Monk did not miss his opportunity. In the excitement when the Sheriff went away, before the questions and the quarrelling began, he reminded his guests that he would have to work through the night, cleaning up the mess they made of the cells, something he had not bargained for. Clearly there must be a surcharge on the admission fees they had already paid. In the exalted mood of the moment, no one demurred and, in the morning, the Monk surprised even his banker with the wad of notes he handed in.

When the new government came to power, things began to go wrong. They wanted to abolish the right of Highlanders to have courts conducted in Gaelic but they were afraid of an appeal to Europe if they proceeded brusquely. Cautiously they declared their passionate attachment to Gaelic but argued that chosing the language in which your case was heard was a personal matter, much the same as chosing the advocate who conducted it for you. They introduced a steep scale of charges for the use of the equipment installed in the Court and decided that no installations would be made in other courts until the need was proven. Of course, they argued, there was no hardship on litigants because the cost of hiring the equipment qualified as a legitimate expense and was covered by the Legal Aid Scheme.

Most of those who qualified for Legal Aid had no political interest in the language. All they wanted was to get through the spot of bother they were in with the least possible hassle. Most of the activists who led the campaign for Gaelic were too well heeled to qualify for Legal Aid but, not unnaturally, just as they demanded Gaelic Courts on principle so they refused to pay for them on principle. The translation machine fell into disuse. The freelance journalists had to return to straightforward or not so straightforward reporting. The Monk had to think of something new.

Tourists still flocked to the Dry Shebeen. It was now, in a sense, more illict than ever for them to be in the Court House at night, behind shuttered windows, using one of the most remarkable machines known to man. The Monk could no longer play them tapes of Gaelic court cases but he gave them recitals of Gaelic poetry, interspersed at times with extracts from the Gaelic Bible, or even sonorous passages from published Gaelic sermons by old divines and passages from Carmina Gadelica. He had a fine baritone voice and clear diction. He got as much satisfaction out of his performances as a diva would, reaching with ease for impossible notes in a difficult opera. He was no longer a glorified janitor. He was a star.

More importantly, a new generation of Gaelic writers saw the opportunity to get their work transmitted across the globe, in more than a score of languages. A new source of income opened up for the Monk when he was offered inducements to include the work of budding poets in his repertoire. As most of the poets wrote for love not money, they were prepared to make a modest payment for access to such an audience. Their simple lines, coming from the heart of a living community, had a profound effect on a whole generation, world wide. It was humanity's answer to the glitz and glitter of Hollywood. A bonfire of the money markets.

The Monk's involvement came to an abrupt end when Sir Thomas Abeckett retired from the civil service and became a director in his nephew's firm. It was then the press spotted what they called the "trail of slime" left by the retiring civil servant, as he moved silently, and as he thought unobserved, from the post in which his influence had created a demand for his nephew's invention to the wealthy firm his influence had thus created. It was true the gigantic market in all the law courts of the world had not been achieved, but there were plenty of other uses for the equipment and the pioneering venture in Carbost, which demonstrated its efficacy, had set the firm securely on its feet.

Sir Thomas explained sincerely and truthfully, to the Government's Committee of Enquiry, that he had no ulterior motive in his mind when he first raised the Pakistani argument against the use of Gaelic in the courts. He had not mentioned his nephew's invention, he had not even realised its potential, until faced with the problem of implementing a policy imposed upon him by (what he called) the pig headedness of the government he served. The more he explained and the more open and truthful he was, the less he was believed.

At that point a Carbost journalist broke the story of the Sheriff's Dry Shebeen. He raised by inference the question was Sir Thomas in on this as well? Did he draw dividends from the Monk's illicit business? Did Sir Thomas plan it all, down to the midnight sessions behind shuttered windows? After all, he knew Carbost well. He had gone there year after year to fish.

The journalist knew there was not a word of truth in the imputation. In fact he had been drinking with the Monk when the idea unexpectedly blossomed from the humorous conversation they were having about the monstrous machine being installed in the Monk's domain. There may have been some envy in the journalist's betrayal of his friend. Why should the Monk have got all the loot?

As soon as the story was out, the authorities moved fast. Sir Thomas had committed no obvious crime, even if his advice to government was tainted, but the Monk had made improper use of government machinery. He had stolen electricity to run his illict business. He was in contempt of court. In breach of the terms of his employment. Above all, he was the ideal scapegoat: a man of no account, who couldn't hit back. As a Scottish judge of an earlier age had put it, he would be none the worse of a hanging.

When the police pounced, the nest was empty. The Monk and his ill gotten gains were safe in the Cayman Islands. He spent the rest of his life wandering from pub to pub, teaching anyone who would drink with him to say "slainte", when he raised his glass. It was the only contact he had with the language he loved but, in a remote forest in Borneo, half a century later, a professor from California gathered material for a learned thesis, on the influence of Gaelic poetry and thought on the oral culture of a hitherto unknown tribe.

Sacrament on Grimsay

THE ISLAND OF GRIMSAY lies in the ocean like the tail of a gigantic dragon. It is little more than a high spiny ridge, with great plates of Lewisian gneiss glittering in the watery sunshine, scales of armour which neither sword nor spear could pierce. Only the fire is missing. The snorting head of the petrified monster, if it ever existed, must lie beneath the waves, well doused by the seas, which roar in from the Atlantic at each extremity, as if trying to encircle Grimsay in a furious embrace.

The main road runs along the east side of the island, well above the sea, but still far below the knobbly summits of the spine; a thin grey line, as if marking an unusually high tide from the Ice Age, like the parallel roads in Glen Roy, or just the play of light along the edge where the monster's side folds over to become his back.

Here and there the road corkscrews down a dizzy gulley to the sea, bumps across a narrow mountain stream by a hump-back bridge and struggles breathlessly up again, over the opposite shoulder, escaping from the darkness and the gloom of the pit between the mountains to the clear air above. The little villages where the crofter fishermen live, or lived, for the island is sadly depopulated, at least of its native stock, are in the sheltered valley bottoms, if that is not too pretentious a description for narrow threads of green, hemmed in, compressed, and throttled by the towering hills.

At the top of the rise above the village of Balmeanach, at the point where the road levels off, the Tourist Association has built a car park and a viewpoint. It is admirably sited because the motorist (and only the motorist is thought of now) can sit in his comfortable saloon, as indolent and uncomprehending as a slug on a cabbage leaf, and see the whole sweep of the Hebrides before him, from the Cuillins to Mull, and, on a clear day, through a cleft between the hills behind him, if he has the energy to turn his head, a glimpse of St Kilda, far to the westward: a small group of diminutive pinnacles, standing up from the rim of the horizon like splintered stumps of teeth protruding from the withered gums of the Atlantic.

Some motorists do leave their cars for a moment or two, attracted by the direction indicator, which identifies the islands and the more prominent of the mountains, but more of them, oddly enough, struggle from their cocoon to look at the blackened ruins of a building just below the viewpoint, where the women especially stand with their heads tilted, listening intently for the fairy fiddle, which a surprising number of them profess to hear. It is not entirely imagination, however, because some trick of the landscape, on the occasional day when the incessant Hebridean gale drops to a breeze, produces a low humming sound which varies in pitch markedly enough to suggest a musical instrument, played in a desultory way, at a remote distance, so that only broken snatches can be heard. To my ear, not unnaturally, in view of the manner in which the sound is produced, it is more reminiscent of a primitive woodwind than a stringed instrument, but it is the only authentic ghostly song I know, and whatever the physical origin or characteristics of the sound, the instrument I hear when I stand there, especially at nightfall, is undoubtedly a violin.

It was Grace Moir who popularised, indeed invented, the legend of the fairy fiddler, although she proudly boasts, and quite honestly believes, that she has merely rescued a treasure from the past. For many years she has lived in Grimsay, in daily conference with the people, exasperated by them on almost every encounter, because of the fundamental difference in their modes of thought, but cherishing her exasperation with the forgiving passion of the early Christian missionary embracing martyrdom with ecstasy. "If you knew their history you would understand," she says to her more forthright visitors, when they feel they have been rebuffed by a crofter, who has misinterpreted what they said, or who has felt his privacy invaded by their brashness, and has courteously tried to fend them off. The truth is that she herself does not really understand, nor indeed does she even know, the crofters' history, for she sees it all through a distorting mirror: the romanticism which brought her to Grimsay in the first place and which has kept her there, like a visitor strayed in from Mars, vainly pretending that he speaks the language and enjoys the climate here on earth although, when he is honest with himself, he realises that he is putting a good face on things, because there is no way now in which he can go home.

Be that as it may, her books sell, possibly because so many visitors to Grimsay have the same basic inability to understand the unfamiliar. They share her readiness to accept a vivid, simple, childish vision of the island, as a poor man's paradise, where the stranger from the real world can rest content and feel superior. The Tourist Association, with the naive cynicism of the commercial mind, alert to the prospect of clicking turnstiles, pounced greedily on the fairy fiddler as soon as she created him. The true story of the haunting is very different and belongs to my early youth. In fact, I have a photograph taken on an old box Brownie at the scene, and at the moment, when it all began. It seemed an ordinary enough snapshot at the time but, while others may fake their plates and still persuade themselves that they have captured the ectoplasm as it emerged from nowhere, I focused on a commonplace rural scene, and discovered, only years afterwards, that I had photographed a haunted community, in the throes of childbirth: the demon who came to inhabit them was in process of being born.

The sepia print is crumpled round the edges and badly faded. It only survived at all because it was a reminder of my first adventure into photography. My father developed the film for me, but I made the print myself, at the kitchen window, in the sun, filled with a wonder, which has never left me, as the miracle was unfolded, and a scene which had ceased to exist, and could never be precisely restored, however carefully one re-enacted it, emerged before my eyes in every detail.

It was many years later I first began to realise how superficial my miracle had been. The faces were there true enough, a reminder for all time of Ruari Mor, a pillar of black granite when he stood erect, his white beard and hair like a wreath of snow or a strange exuberant lichen, clinging to the rock: and Ruari Beag, his antithesis and brother, a little black terrier, or an eel, writhing and darting at the other's feet: the one ponderous, massive, rigid and upright, the other with a mind that moved, like his body, in tongues and flashes of fire. I often wondered whether they represented the two aboriginal strains whose fusion made Grimsay what it was, the Norseman and the Celt, inextricably interwoven for a score of generations, then suddenly unravelled and delivered, strangely resolved into the constituent elements, from one womb. The fancy was reinforced by the fact that Ruari Mor was a seaman, supreme in a gale with the tiller in his hand, while Ruari Beag was a herdsman, unrivalled with sheep.

It was Ruari Beag's day when I took the photograph. I caught a moment of stillness from the uproar of a fank; frozen immobility, as unrepresentative of the scene as anything could be, but which still, such is the power of the human imagination, recalls the welter of sound from dogs and sheep, men and women, and above all children, bustling excitedly in and around the muddy confines of the drystone dyke, as the sheep were hunted, cornered, and dragged to the dipper on slithering feet, then plunged protesting into an evil-smelling fluid, of which even the stench assails me when memory is triggered by the fading print.

Also in the picture was Seonaid Thorcuil, who was our immediate neighbour when I holidayed in Grimsay with my grandaunt: a squat, pugnacious woman, whose bounty, restricted only by the ultimate limit of her resources, was thrust on me with a positive, expansive, outgoing generosity that was almost a form of violence. I was often rescued by my grandaunt from a surfeit of Seonaid's fresh-baked bannocks, when my distress had become unbearable, like a recusant snatched from his inquisitors as they try to show their loving care for his immortal soul by tearing his limbs apart.

The smell of these fresh-baked bannocks, which I loved until they became too many for a child to stomach, rise from the print when I look at Seonaid, as clearly as the repellent smells of the fank; and oddly, the two smells can exist, separately but contemporaneously, within my memory, both recalled by a piece of pasteboard, which has no discernible smell of its own, unless it be a faint whiff of age and damp.

In the top corner of the picture, on the left, is another figure, distinct from the others in attitude as in dress: trim, business-like, self-assured, in knickerbockers, leggings, and tweed hat; aloof but still dominant, commanding the attention, although not the affection, of all the rest.

John Martin, the Factor, was not concerned with the fank in any way, although over dinner in the evening he would probably give the impression that he had been there to make sure that everything was going well with the crofters, whose real interests he watched over "more effectively than they could do themselves". In fact, he was there because it was a good opportunity to catch the members of the Township Committee together, to tell them that he intended to resume into the estate's own hands a small corner of their common grazings "just a few acres of worthless bog, you know" to provide a site for a house and a garden. "It's a great thing for Balmeanach," he assured them, "that a man as distinguished as David Prozen has chosen to come among you. He visited Sir George last summer, and he was so taken with the view from the hill above Balmeanach, nothing would satisfy him but that he should have a home where he can come when he wishes quietness to compose."

Apart from the convenience of getting the people he wished to speak to in one spot together, the Factor had in mind that they would be anxious to get on with the work in hand, and would not be so inclined to argue as they sometimes were, "over trifles, you know: they magnify the smallest things out of all proportion." "It's such a miserable piece of grazing it's not worth claiming compensation for," he told the Grazings Committee. "I'll send the papers out by post. If we get it settled by consent, it will save time and trouble. Besides, Mr Prozen is desperately keen to get started on the building. His architect will be here next week."

Without a word, the members of the committee returned to their work, as soon as the Factor had spoken. They made no sign or comment to each other, but went on steadily with the work. It was at that moment, when the Factor paused on the fringe of the crowd, his mission completed as he thought that I pressed the button on my camera.

If Martin had not been so anxious to catch the crofters off their guard, he might have talked them into agreement. The piece of grazings involved was not completely worthless, as the Factor had said, but its loss would not have required the reduction of the village sheep stock by a single ewe; and knowledge of who David Prozen was and, more importantly, a meeting with him, if it could have been arranged, would probably have removed any prejudice against a stranger, or rather against the idea of a stranger.

If David Prozen had walked into any house in the village and asked for a cup of tea, he would have got it. Even if he did not ask, it would have been offered to him, before anyone took the trouble to enquire although they would, eventually and persistently, though circumspectly, who he was, and what had brought him to Balmeanach. The tradition of the township was to keep an open door for strangers, all strangers, and to enjoy their company as a break in the monotony of life.

But Prozen had not come to them as a stranger: he came to them as a ghost, unseen, impalpable, a name only, and used by the man in whom, less than in anyone else, they were prepared to trust. Not that Martin had ever seriously betrayed them, but he was the descendant, in a historical and institutional sense, of all that they had learned to fear in the past. Martin, as a man, they rather liked, but when he spoke as Factor, his voice was distorted and menacing, amplified, not by electronic gadgetry such as the youth of today use to deafen themselves and shut out reality, but by the reverberations of a long folk-memory, still raw and sensitive, ready to be awakened by the lightest touch.

They now had security of tenure, to a very considerable degree. They could no longer be removed from their crofts and their homes at the whim of landlord or factor. Even the abstraction from their grazings of a little piece of land, for Prozen's house, would require the sanction of the Land Court, and they were accustomed to pleading their cause before the Court, often without the aid of a legal adviser. The Court was informal and accessible, prepared to sit in the village church or school, to bring justice close to the people, and to go out on the ground with the crofters, and have the matter explained to them with a great deal of gesticulation and pointing, and appeals from one crofter to another to corroborate an assertion or a fact. The crofters enjoyed an argument before the Court, even when they were not seriously concerned about the outcome: it was part of the ritual dance which celebrated their freedom, and the Factor's attempt to shorten, or perhaps avoid, the Court procedure, touched them on the raw.

It was Ruari Beag who first gave voice to their fears. "Why does he want to rush us?" he said to Norman Finlayson, the Clerk to the Township Committee, when they brushed past each other in the never-ending movement of the fank.

"Why, indeed?" replied Norman.

Neither of them paused, and nothing more was said, but in two minds, by that brief exchange, suspicion became certainty. Norman, a merry soul who laughed his way through life like a kettle briskly on the boil, with sudden snorts of steam and spats of water, had probably no suspicion of his own until Ruari Beag implanted it, but his very guilelessness made him fertile soil for fear to flourish in.

Ruari Mor asked no questions, hypothetical or otherwise. He had gone off silently, working over the Factor's statement in his mind. With a memory still accustomed to an oral tradition and unencumbered with trivial reading, he could remember every word as it had been uttered, the tone in which it was said, and the expression on the Factor's face as he spoke. His observation was precise, accurate, and, like his character, inflexible. No one could ever convince him afterwards that a word he had heard had not been spoken, or that a word spoken had not been seriously intended, or even that there was any scope for misunderstanding between listener and speaker. When he passed Norman, a little later than his brother, he said simply, "We will resist!"

Although these messages were exchanged without interrupting the work of the fank, the arrival of the Factor and his summons to the members of the committee had aroused curiosity and everyone who rubbed shoulders, in the course of the day, with one of the chosen group, had a brief question to ask and received a brief but adequate answer: adequate, that is, to satisfy his curiosity, and transform it into anger. The brevity of the answers, like the abruptness of the Factor's visit, gave urgency to something which might otherwise have aroused much less excitement.

It was almost as if I had photographed the community at the onset of an epidemic, when the germs of flu or plague! had struck the early victims and begun to spread but had not yet revealed their presence by any obvious physical effects.

In a sense, it was worse than an epidemic, worse even than an uncontrolled fire. Fire cannot burn the same thing twice. Even an epidemic builds up resistance in its victims, and eventually disarms itself, but an idea, a fear, a rumour, creates no antibodies as it leaps from mind to mind. Unlike a fading echo, each reverberation reinforces those which have gone before. A man who is only half convinced, when he gives voice to a vague fear, is carried over any hump of doubt by the impetus of his own words, spoken in his ear by someone else a few hours later, when the circuit is complete. He does not recognise them as his own because, in the interval, the fear has been given shape and substance by imaginative minds, less disciplined to truth than his, and authenticity by the very caution of those who have passed it on with precision, just as it had come to them.

"He's a foreigner." "He's a Jew." "He's fleeing from justice and wants a quiet place to hide." "He's only the first." "Open the door and they'll come in a flood." "There's a list in the Factor's office as long as my arm." "There's a foreign company behind it." "They've bought the whole island but they're not letting on." "It's the grazings today, it'll be the crofts tomorrow." "My grandmother's house was burnt over her head."

By nightfall, the village was no longer concerned with a house for David Prozen, nor had they any interest in knowing who he was. They were fighting over again the battles of an earlier generation, which did not have their legal apparatus of defence, determined to resist, simply to demonstrate they had the power to do so, and to resist with passion, because their ancestors had been defenceless and abused.

When Norman Finalyson eventually received the Factor's letter, he was puzzled to know what to do with it. He had been the most passionate among them when the villagers discussed the disaster which seemed to threaten them, although it was quite unreal, and entirely different from the disaster which did threaten them and which, in part, they were preparing for themselves; but alone, in the presence of the Factor's friendly and persuasive letter, his natural guilelessness reasserted itself, and almost brought him to the truth.

The letter thanked the crofters for listening to him so patiently, and for the agreement they had reached. The writer was sure the village would benefit greatly through having a distinguished violinist and composer like David Prozen as their neighbour and, he hoped, their friend, as he was himself.

Although Martin did not realise it when he wrote, that last plausible, ingratiating phrase, attempting to get Prozen accepted on the strength of his own imagined popularity, would have condemned him with most of the crofters, even if there had been nothing else. As Ruari Beag put it, "We don't want the Factor's spy sitting up there with a telescope, looking on at every move we make."

Norman, however, accepted it all at its face value. He was so innocent that, even if he had known how famous Prozen really was, he would have missed the little bit of snobbery in the Factor's attempt to link his own name with the composer's. The point, which lodged in Norman's mind, was the Factor's assertion that an agreement had been reached. Had they really agreed? Or, what was more likely, had they given the Factor the impression they had agreed, and so entered into a moral commitment from which they would have difficulty in pulling honourably back? The formal document was there, all ready for their signatures, with a mark to show where they should put their names. There was even a stamped addressed envelope so that it would cost them nothing to return the completed document.

"I think I should call a meeting of the committee so that we can make up our minds about the Factor's paper," he said tentatively to Ruari Mor, whom he had gone to consult. Although he was still under the influence of his own easy-going inclination to accept the so-called agreement, with a wry laugh at their own incompetence as bargainers, rather than get involved in all the bother of resistance, he began to feel the granite force of Ruari's character, as he approached his house, even before they actually met.

Ruari brushed the proffered envelope aside. "We will resist," he said simply, just as he had done on the first occasion.

"It's the Factor's letter," said Norman, tendering it to him again.

"I am not concerned with the Factor's letter," said Ruari. "We have made up our minds."

"What should I say to him in reply?" asked Norman.

"You will not reply!" said Ruari. "We will resist."

"We will have to give some reply. He has sent us a stamped envelope," said Norman.

"If he wants to waste his stamps, that's his business," said Ruari Mor, turning to walk away. He was stopped by his brother, who had just joined them.

"Do you want to make a thief of Norman?" asked Ruari Beag, half closing his eyes to repress a smile, as if trying to contain the little bit of malevolent fun which was taking shape behind them. "Stealing the poor man's stamps," he added, by way of explanation.

Ruari Mor waved his hand impatiently. He had little time for his brother's devious approach. Ruari Beag, he used to say, could reach a conclusion quicker than any other man in the village, but it was always the wrong one, and if, by chance, it was the right one, he got it by the wrong road. And yet, the brothers liked and admired each other. The difference in their mode of thought was superficial, like a little bit of patterning around an edge, giving individuality to the respective contributions they made to the strong bond of affection, indeed love, which held them together as a family.

Quick as a flash, Ruari Beag changed his tactics as he sensed his brother's annoyance. The playful light in his eyes went out and he spoke directly to the point. "We will call a meeting of the whole township. The committee is not enough. We will read the Factor's letter, every last word of it. We will then burn the letter, and the papers, and send the ashes back to him in his own envelope."

"That would be the waste of a good match," said Norman. In the presence of the brothers' firmness his own doubts had disappeared, but he was not as quick as Ruari Beag in adjusting to the older man's solemn mood.

"If you are quick with the match you can light your pipe with it, after you've burnt the papers," said Ruari Beag, once more responding quickly to a changing situation. He knew, although nothing was said, that Ruari Mor now accepted his seriousness, and his will to resist, even if he had reservations about the way their resolve should be expressed: the important thing was to stiffen Norman up, and that could best be done by exploiting the humour of the situation.

"For that matter," said Norman, responding to the lead, "we can pass the paper round as it burns and light every pipe in the village."

"Yes," said Ruari Beag, "and then you'll write and tell him what you've done. He can put that in his pipe and smoke it!"

"There's a stamp on the Factor's paper, as well as the envelope. For us to write our names across. If I burn the stamp, will I be a thief or a fire raiser?" said Norman, whose fear of the Factor, and whose acceptance of his assurances, had alike vanished in a riot of fun.

"You'll steam it off and send it back to him in the envelope with the ashes," said Ruari Beag, adding, as another thought struck him "He can use it then for the next paper he sends us."

"Call a meeting of the whole village. I agree to that," said Ruari Mor, cutting short their banter. Without another word, he left them.

At the meeting, the fiercest attack on Prozen came from Maclachlan, the minister, who did not normally attend village meetings and, when he did, generally sided with the Factor or with whatever other authority was involved.

"Do you realise that this man is a vain fiddler?" he demanded. "A foreigner, a Jew and an Englishman? He not only plays the instrument himself, in concert halls, and theatres, and other temples of Satan, he composes secular songs to infect the minds of other people!"

In a great welter of words and waving of arms, which had all the irrational, destructive fury of a storm at sea, Maclachlan accused the man who, if he had lived, might have become the greatest composer of the twentieth century, as a tempter, a suborner, a seducer, a pervert, a man of immense power and yet of no consequence; a materialist prepared to sell his own and other people's souls for money; an idler, who frittered away his time like a butterfly; a Marxist and an agent of the Pope; an anarchist whose songs were more deadly than bombs or poison gas; a serpent in Eden; a harlot like Jezebel, and a betrayer of his Lord like Judas Iscariot.

Some of the crofters accepted every word Maclachlan said. They saw their own unspotted lives in danger from a creeping fungus which could blight their happiness in this life and condemn them to everlasting torment in the life to come. Others were bludgeoned into acquiescence by the drum-beat of the preacher's phrases, without understanding a word he said. A few were uneasy because the extravagance of the language brought them face to face with the real facts. It exposed their lack of knowledge of the man they were condemning. The minister's fears were absurd, and that brought home to them that their own were insubstantial. His were inflamed by fantasy while theirs rested, just as insecurely, on ignorance.

Ruari Beag sought refuge in laughter. He wanted to whisper to someone, "If the fiddler set the minister to music, what a winner it would be!" but when he looked around he could see no ear within his reach into which it was safe to be irreverent.

His brother was more deeply concerned. The minister sounded so like a parody of his own opposition to the unknown stranger, he began to have doubts, but he did not change course easily, and sought refuge in action. Before the minister spoke, they were all agreed that they should resist the Factor's demand, but there were so many different opinions as to the way in which they should show their opposition, there was a risk their resolution would run into the sand, like a river splitting up at the end of its majestic course into a delta of sluggish, muddy channels, meandering, without purpose, towards their own extinction. Ruari Beag had also seen the danger and passed a note to his brother along the row of desks in the schoolroom where they met. It said simply, "For God's sake, give them a lead."

All through the minister's oration, Ruari Mor had pondered the matter, and he was ready to rise as soon as the minister ran out of steam.

"I will go to Edinburgh at my own expense," he said. "I will find the best lawyer in Scotland to write to the Factor for us. He will tell him we are not parting with an inch of land for any friend of his. If he goes to the Land Court, the lawyer will fight for us there. And if we lose, we will camp on the ground in turns, night after night, until they get the soldiers to drive us out." "Besides," he added, somewhat to his own surprise, "the land is not worthless as the Factor says. It could easily be drained and put under grass. You will start tomorrow on the drains, and, when I am on the mainland, I will buy the seeds and fertilisers and the fencing posts."

For years, the Factor had been pressing them to reclaim that very bog, and Ruari Mor himself had been the most stubborn in his opposition, because his interest was in the sea rather than the land. In a sense, he was turning his coat because it suited him, but he was also making a real sacrifice in the interests of the village because he, having very little stock, would derive no benefit from the expenditure, although he would have to bear his share of it.

"What will we use it for?" asked one of the crofters. It was a dangerous question. Many of them, like Ruari Mor, had little stock. Others carried more than the number they were entitled to. On which figure should their contribution be based? Some had only sheep, and would wish to use the reclaimed land purely for grazing. Others had cattle with a need for hay or silage, if the grass could be mowed.

The meeting might have got into an argument about township management, as remote from their real purpose as the minister's tirade had been, but the danger was averted by Norman Finlayson. He did not actually see the danger, but he could not resist the chance of raising a laugh.

"We'll make a bull park of it," he said. "The Factor can give his next paper to the bull."

The picture of the village bull parading around the battlefield, keeping the Factor and his friends at bay, appealed to them so greatly, they all trooped out in high spirits, exchanging with each other, as they went, a hundred different scenarios of the situation which might result.

Ruari Beag winked at Norman across the classroom, and flung him a box of matches. Norman took the point and, holding the Factor's letter by one corner, as if it were unclean, applied a symbolic unlit match to it. He had no intention of burning it, but Ruari Mor was taking no chances. He snatched it from him saying, "I will need that for the lawyer, and the other papers too."

"What the devil has got into them?" said the Factor testily, when his stamped addressed envelope eventually came back to him, from a firm of solicitors in Edinburgh, with a curt note expressing the crofters' refusal to release the land. It was anaemic compared with the letter the crofters themselves might have written, or would have wished their solicitor to write, if they had been consulted as to its terms, but it had a much more profound effect on Martin than any intemperate bluster. He had ridden out the crofters' storms before, and come through triumphant, but this was the real thing. "They have more money than sense, spending it on lawyer's fees," he told his wife at lunch time, and then he added petulantly, "If they can afford a firm like Gemmel and Mason, they can afford higher rents."

A few days later, one of the estate staff reported that the crofters were "working like navvies" digging drains in the bog above Balmeanach.

Martin realised then that he had been outwitted. He had swithered whether or not to go to the Land Court, despite the crofters' opposition. He had got housing sites in the past, elsewhere on the estate, against their wishes, but that had been for public housing schemes for the local population, and the land had been specially suitable, having regard to roads and other services. Here he was seeking a comparatively large site for one house, for a person who would use it only as an occasional retreat and, although it was reasonably near the road, the other services would have to be provided at considerable cost. Indeed, he would not have got outline planning permission but for the fact that the members of the local authority were more pliable than the crofters, when a man in Martin's position went quietly to work on them. He came eventually to the conclusion that a rebuff in the Land Court would stiffen the resistance of the crofters elsewhere in Grimsay, and in the other islands of the estate, and he could not risk that, because he had plans to promote the building of holiday homes on quite a large scale, in areas sufficiently far from a salmon river or deer forest to be safe; a method of selection which threw them towards the crofting townships where the loss of land would be most keenly felt. He must find some other way of breaking the stubborn fools in Balmeanach.

He came close to throwing in his hand to avoid a confrontation but he realised that that would be seen by the crofters as an even cheaper victory than they had expected, whatever explanation he invented, such as his client's change of mind, or his sudden departure for a world concert tour. Besides, he did not want to confess to his employer that he was unable to persuade the crofters. The loss of face with his landlord was much more serious than a loss of face with the tenants, which troubled him not at all, apart from the practical consequences.

In the end, he decided to go to Balmeanach to inspect the reclamation work and congratulate the crofters on their enterprise. He would sound them out obliquely and perhaps even persuade them to change their minds, he told his wife, but he did not entertain high hopes of that, and his real purpose was to check some facts on the ground, which were relevant to his new strategy. "They've chosen to fight, but I'll choose the weapons," he said grimly to himself.

He was impressed with the work the crofters were doing, and congratulated them with genuine warmth. He even invited them to drink a pint with him afterwards to toast their success, in the Balmeanach Inn, which stood just below the main road, quite close to the area the crofters were working in. Some of them accepted, some did not. Although they were at loggerheads with the Factor over the house site, none of them refused on personal grounds but, small though the village was, it covered the complete spectrum from the inveterate alcoholic to teetotallers whose aversion to liquor was even more compelling than the drunkards' love of it, and perhaps equally rooted in frailty.

Ruari Mor thanked the Factor for his invitation, but excused himself. He was not one of the fanatics, but he was by temperament solitary rather than sociable. The trivial gossip of the bar irritated him even more than the gossip of scandal-bearing women. Besides, having lost a whole week's fishing while on his visit to the city, and several days more while helping with the reclamation, he had no time to spare. He was going to sea on the evening tide.

Ruari Beag, on the other hand, accepted the invitation with alacrity, and walked with the Factor down to the inn, at the head of a straggling line of crofters, for whom the pleasure of the drink was enhanced by the knowledge that the price of it came out of their enemy's pocket. Ruari Beag was, perhaps, more truly temperate than his brother. He could take a social drink or go happily without. He would have accepted an invitation from the Factor, as a matter of diplomacy, at any time, but on this particular occasion he had something to celebrate, because the reclamation was directly to his interest and would make the management of his sheep easier and more profitable. He knew the sacrifice Ruari Mor had made to help with a project from which he would not benefit.

"The Factor is up to something," he whispered to his brother before they parted. "I want to find out what it is."

"You don't need to make excuses to me I never grudged a man a pint," said Ruari Mor. "Keep your explanations for the minister."

It was not often he cracked a joke of any sort, let alone one directed against the minister's intemperate addiction to temperance, but he was in an unusually jovial mood: his little talk with the Factor convinced him that they had won their fight and, unlike his brother, he had no apprehension of further trouble brewing.

On the way to the inn, Ruari Beag and the Factor chatted amicably about the weather, the crops, the condition of the sheep, and the state of the market, and when they had exhausted these topics of immediate concern, they went on to discuss the general news of the day. Martin was always surprised at how well informed the crofters were, and their pithy way of making a point. They often furnished him with a good quote with which, the origin concealed, and the language suitably modified, he could regale the banker and his other professional friends. Once, when he was praised for some particularly lively comment, he waved the compliment aside, remarking, in a rare moment of self-knowledge, "It's just that I'm good at polishing stones. I find them here and there." His interlocutor had no idea what he was getting at, and thought it another example of the Factor's ready wit as, in this case it really was.

When they crowded into the bar, the Factor ordered drinks all round and gave the toast, "To the greatest conversion since Paul saw the light on the road to Damascus!"

Most of the crofters looked blankly at each other, wondering what on earth the Factor meant, but Ruari Beag laughed heartily.

"Paul's conversion was spiritual," he said. "Ours has to do with the autumn sheep sales. The ground was not worth bothering with before, but it is now, with the price of mutton rising."

Ruari had been preaching to the crofters for some time that it would pay them to reclaim the land, just as the Factor had been, but he knew quite well that it wasn't the price of mutton, or his own persuading, that had got them out with spades in their hands.

"Very shrewd, very shrewd," said Martin. "but, now that the job is safely done, or so far on there's no going back, I might as well tell you I have no intention of taking that ground for a house site, and never had. Every time I pass this way and look at the green sward where there used to be heather, I'll smile to myself and whisper, 'There are more ways than one of killing a cat.'"

The crofters were crowding round, listening to every word. Some of them jumped to the conclusion they had been tricked. The Factor's duplicity they accepted: it was natural to the species. It was different with Ruari Beag. He had obviously been in the plot with the Factor all along, to make them dig these bloody drains.

"I don't have much time for anyone who'll do that to his own brother. Think of all the fishing days Ruari Mor lost to fatten that little bastard's sheep." It was Shonnie Ishbel who first gave words to it. His hatred of work was proportionate to his love of liquor, and he was still smarting under all the nudging, cajoling, and bullying he had suffered, as the other crofters compelled him to do his fair share of the digging.

Ruari Beag did not hear the comment, but he sensed the mood. "The reclamation won't put a penny in your pocket, or the landlord's," he said to the Factor loudly, so that everyone would hear him. "You cannot rent us on our own improvements."

"True, true!" said the Factor. "But rent is not everything. We are interested in the welfare of our tenants. We like to see them prosper."

That, as it happened, was the truth. The landlord did like to see his tenants getting on, so long as it wasn't at his expense. Unlike some landlords, he had no envy of the underdog when he began to climb. The crofters, however, judged the landlord and his motives by their own established folk-lore, rather than objective facts. The Factor's comment did not ring true to them, but it helped to convince them that there had been no conspiracy between him and Ruari Beag as, for a moment, they had supposed.

The Factor refused all offers to return his hospitality, explaining that he had actually come to make one of his periodic inspections of the landlord's property, and must hurry if he was not to lose the last of the light. The crofters solemnly raised their glasses behind his retreating back and drank, in whispers so that he could not hear, to their victory over him and the hated foreigner.

"He's putting a good face on it," said Shonnie Ishbel, nodding in the Factor's direction. He expressed the general view, but the remark was really made to draw attention to the fact that his glass was empty and no one had stood him a second drink.

Ruari Beag disagreed. "It's a smokescreen," he said, still wondering what was in the Factor's mind.

After he left them, Martin had paused for several minutes at the bar window, looking out on the mainland hills marching across his line of vision like gigantic soldiers, blue-cloaked in the gathering dusk: and there was a smile lurking round his lips when he went through to the office, to begin a more than usually thorough study of the hotel books, followed by a careful inspection of the whole building.

In the morning he wrote a letter. He had been thinking the matter over, he told Sir George. Building costs were high in the isles, and there seemed little point in letting David Prozen involve himself in the expense of erecting a new house when there was a cheaper method of meeting his requirements, with greater profit to the estate. Balmeanach Inn had almost precisely the same view as the site which Prozen wanted. The inn had no long-term future. It was too small to be a profitable hotel, too large for a village pub. Besides, the crofters were getting fewer, and most of them poorer. He knew Sir George had supported the inn out of the goodness of his heart, as a social amenity but, after all, it was an amenity for casual visitors rather than for his tenants. The crofters did not want tourists roaming all over their grazings, disturbing the stock, and the hardship for them would be greater now that they were reclaiming the land immediately beside the inn. The disturbance caused to stock by visitors was the basis of their rather stupid opposition to David Prozen, whose eminence in the world of music they did not understand, but even the crofters would see that it was to their advantage to have one person using the building as a home, rather than a succession of drouthy tourists looking for a drink, some of them early enough to disturb the lambing. Besides, although he was not averse to taking a social drink himself, and he knew Sir John was the same, it had to be acknowledged that the crofters did not control their drinking so successfully. The inn was the cause of a great deal of over-indulgence in the village. The minister and some of his elders, supported by many of the women of the township, had organised petitions more than once, asking for its closure. He thought their wish should be granted. As to the suitability of the inn for conversion to a private house, he had been over it very carefully; it was structurally sound and the accommodation matched, fairly closely, Prozen's stated needs.

Sir John was doubtful when he got the letter. It was not like the Factor to be quite so considerate of the tenancy, and he suspected some hidden motive, but it seemed a sensible proposition. Rather tentatively, he broached the matter to Prozen, who was delighted. The inn had character. It was more attractive than any modern house. It might even have a ghost, and what could be better for a musician in search of inspiration than a supernatural audience to keep him on his toes? He was so pleased he wrote the Factor direct, "God bless you, John, for the idea," a familiarity which led Martin to amend his standard reference to "David Prozen you know, the violinist and composer." It now became "my friend, David Prozen you know, THE David Prozen."

The news hit Balmeanach like a bomb, simultaneously disrupting the community and uniting it, in a frenzy of destruction: a demonstration of violence which would not have been possible if the community itself had not been the victim as well as the agent.

Martin's prediction that the crofters would be pleased to have one stranger to cope with instead of a succession was quickly disproved. Ordinary tourists came and went like birds of passage. They might be a nuisance at times, but they were a feature of the island, which use and wont had hallowed: accepted like the weather, even when it was execrated. Prozen, a foreigner imposed on them by trickery, a symbol of the fact that, even when the law was on the crofters' side and their grazings could not be tampered with, unless the Court agreed, the power of the landlord was such that he could flout their wishes, and stab them in the back. If Prozen had been evil incarnate, he could not have stirred up more animosity. The fact that they had no idea of his physical appearance helped them to recreate him in monstrous shapes. The minister's attack on his profession came back to their minds, exaggerated and distorted, even beyond his power of self-hallucination and abuse.

The minister's own first reaction was to welcome the closing of the pub as the work of the Lord, but then he was reminded that, according to himself, Prozen and his vain music was a greater evil than alcohol. He went round in a state of confusion, welcoming the one and denouncing the other, seeing the developing situation as an apocalyptic struggle between God and Satan. Right would triumph in the end. Of that he was sure. The closing of the hated pub was earnest of it. But the devil was far from being subdued.

The topers in the village, and even those who liked an occasional social drink, were furious that their one amenity was being withdrawn to serve the wishes of the Factor's friend, and the minister's ambivalent eloquence added to their animosity towards Prozen and the Factor because it gave them, for the first time, a legitimate external object for the hidden hatred which they had for the Church's repressive activities, and which, in normal times, they had to hide, even from themselves, because of the strength of custom and observance.

Even the two Ruaris and Norman Finlayson lost much of their normal poise and gave way to unaccustomed bouts of passion. They knew that, if the pub was closed, drinking would continue in other ways, less easily controlled. The thought that the Factor was prepared to impose bothans and sheebeens on the village, in order to score a victory over them, destroyed even the qualified respect they formerly had for him. He was astonished, on his next visit to the village, to see the three men, quite independently, turn their backs on him and walk away, without returning his greeting, when he came to speak to them.

The work of converting the inn progressed but slowly. None of the villagers would accept employment although they needed the money. The workers eventually scraped together from other parts of the island, were not of the best, and were subject to continual jeering and even harassment by the Balmeanach folk, because of their involvement with evil.

When Prozen himself came up to inspect progress, he was met by a palpable wall of hatred which he could not break. On his earlier visit he had found the villagers friendly, even though they had no idea who he was; now they treated him like a pariah. Breaking all their own traditions, they even shut their doors in his face, once they had learned to recognise him.

"I cannot understand it," he told the Factor. "I formed the impression that this was a friendly place. That was one of the things that attracted me. I felt there was an atmosphere here in which my music could flower, an ambience of humanity, of place, and order, and community; something positive, and quite apart from the absence of the city's distractions, important though that can be. Where have I gone wrong?" he asked, as if almost pleading for comfort.

It startled the Factor to hear the composer assume to himself even the possibility of a fault. He mistook the humility of a great man for softness or was it guile? He did not know. He could not possibly understand. In the same situation, he would have revelled in the crofters' opposition. He liked to be on good terms with his tenants, because it was the simplest way of getting them to do what he wanted, but, if he did quarrel with them, it was a challenge to his manhood, which steeled his determination to succeed, even if, in the interval, he had come to suspect a little uneasily that right was on their side. Prozen was different. He was shy, sensitive, introspective. He was unmoved by other people's view of him, but responsive to it. Lonely, detached, completely resolute in pursuing his own artistic purpose, but always smarting from imagined slights or fears of his own inadequacy. He shunned crowds, even small groups, and yet to appear on the concert platform before a vast audience, rising to acclaim him, was the great joy of his life, second only to the joy of realising suddenly, in the isolation of his study, that he had set down on the paper before him a few silent hieroglyphs which resolved a problem of composition with which he had been wrestling; hieroglyphs which, translated into sound, would give joy for years, perhaps even centuries, to the select few who really understood music, because they knew by experience the difficulties with which it had to cope, as well as the resolutions it achieved. He winced when people made flattering remarks about his work, but he hated still more the slightest trace of indifference, even from people he had never met before and would never meet again, such as a slovenly shop-girl, greasy with make-up, and obviously bored with the first day's work in an empty lifetime, who failed to see him, let alone to return his little smile, as she handed him a morning paper or a packet of cigarettes, with a gesture of weary disdain. Where others would have laughed, or been furious, he was hurt! He went through life as if he had been flayed: craving nothing so much as the comfort of a healing hand, but so raw and sensitive that the slightest touch was agony.

"It's a small matter," the Factor told him with a dismissive shrug. "The trouble comes from a tiny minority the alcoholics. You've deprived them of their pub."

"Me?" said Prozen with astonishment. It had not occurred to him before, there was no reason why it should, that the conversion of the old inn into a dwelling house involved the closing of the only licensed premises on the island. If he had given it any thought, he would have assumed that the estate were closing the old inn to open a more efficient one elsewhere. The thought that he had deprived even a small section of the community, of a legitimate pleasure, or even a destructive solace sought in desperation, appalled him. "It is too late to stop," he said despairingly, thinking of the work now rapidly reaching a conclusion, and the furniture already on its way by rail and steamer. "Like a spider's web," he said, a little cryptically. "Fine threads in a fragile coherence. I have blown it away. The community is destroyed."

Martin laughed. It was meant to be reassuring, but he found Prozen's sensitivity so absurdly funny the laugh was uncontrolled and mocking. "You under-rate them. They will soon make their own arrangements. The drouths will have their dram. The teetotallers will have their self-righteousness. In a few months they'll have forgotten that the inn ever existed."

"What about me?" said Prozen. "I cannot work in an atmosphere of hate. I want people to leave me alone, but I do not want them to shun me. I want to be one of them, to feel them around me, to write their humanity into my music. They have the qualities we have destroyed in our great stone deserts. I want to rediscover the secret and celebrate it. How can I, if I am shut out from it as a stranger, an intruder, an enemy, a thief?"

"You will be just as popular with the teetotallers as you are unpopular with the drouths," said the Factor. "It all balances out."

"Balance! balance! balance!" said Prozen impatiently. "It is not balance. It is not weighing an ounce of love against an ounce of hate, in cold steel scales, with a swinging arm. It is a seamless robe or it is nothing. It is the sense that the drunkards belong to the sober and the sober to the drunkards, that everyone has his place and purpose in the same community, that they all love, or at least accept, even when they condemn: that is what I want to write music about, and for. That is the harmony this world has lost, the harmony of dissonance within an agreed frame, the acceptance of differences as enrichment of all, instead of an occasion for envy, and meanness and destruction.

"The notes I write on the page have order and form and balance, but that is not the music. The music is a chaos inside me, which is real and non-existent at the same time; it is complete and stable and permanent, if only I can hold it, but it is writhing in my hands like a myriad ghostly serpents. The harder I clutch, the less I grasp. But eventually the swelling cloud becomes the glittering star; the stars take up position in the constellations, and the constellations in the firmament, all different in size, and brilliance, and age, and distance, different in their substance too, if we analyse them with the spectroscope, but all moving with a majestic rhythm, – the silent harmony of the night.

"A real community has this harmony too, like music in the mind of God, and people write it down in their work, and their games, their love-making, their quarrels, their funerals, their feasts; or perhaps it exists in the collective mind of the people themselves, so that the music is there from the start, struggling to play itself out in the lives of those who are part of it, but are not conscious of the fact.

"As an artist, I fight for my individual freedom, my integrity, my irresponsibility. I delude myself. As a single note, I am insignificant, worthless, unnoticed. I only exist in relationship with other people. It is the music that is real, not the notes. It is not whether I am me that matters, but whether I am part of a mob: inchoate, unrelated, dissonant, swirling atoms of discontent, colliding, repulsing, affecting each other, but never relating in any stable or coherent way; or whether I am part of a harmony of people complex, perhaps incomprehensible, fragile, possibly unstable, but with the power to change, unfold, adapt, survive. Here, in little, under the microscope, I found what I have wanted to study, and to write in harmonies which might heal the world, and now it is spoiled, as if some blundering oaf had bumped the table, so that slides, and specimens, and microscope, are all in fragments on the floor."

Martin was quite worried by this time at the frenzy Prozen had worked himself into. "God, the man is mad," he said later, to the banker. "I have never heard such balderdash in my life," he said, a little more moderately, to his wife, adding, with a self-satisfied smile, "I solved his problem for him, of course. I told him how to get at the islanders through their stomachs and their pockets, but I did not put it to him quite like that. I hope, in the end of the day, he finds what he's looking for, though heaven knows what it is!"

It was as a result of the Factor's advice that every resident in Balmeanach, including the minister and the school children, was invited to an 'At Home', in the inn, to meet their new neighbour. The villagers were puzzled to know what an 'At Home' was, but the schoolmaster told them it would probably be a "ceilidh with the guts out, the sort of stiff, prim, cup-of-tea, shake hands and go, which you would expect from the English."

There was great discussion in the village about the course to pursue, and everyone was agreed that the 'At Home' should be avoided like the plague, half of them because they did not want to sup with the devil, however long the spoon, and the other half because it promised to be too non-alcoholic for their comfort.

In the end, of course, everyone went, including the minister, to whom Prozen had gone in person, to ask him to say grace before their meal.

"If Satan is trying to use me for his own purpose, I will show that I can bend his purpose to ends of my own," he said to Ruari Mor when he asked him to go along for moral support. "With a little assistance from God, no doubt," said Ruari dryly, having noted, and disapproved, the minister's arrogance, but he went with him obediently.

The evening began tamely enough. The minister said grace at considerable length, and with many crude innuendoes, about the purpose of their gathering, which did not offend Prozen only because Maclachlan, with more discretion than courtesy, addressed the Almighty in a language which the host did not understand.

Then they had tea, with cakes and sandwiches in abundance, although the crofters looked askance at the under-nourished fragments of bread, which they had difficulty in grasping in their massive, calloused paws.

"I know now how they divided the loaves and fishes between five thousand," whispered Norman Finlayson to Ruari Beag, as he picked up a sandwich at the third attempt. The remark was not intended to be offensive, or even critical, unlike the grace: Norman, although not entirely at his ease, was anxious to extract from the evening the greatest possible amount of fun.

"It's only the loaves we're getting, and not much of them," responded Ruari. "Maybe we'll go for the fishes when the party's over." A remark which, if he had overheard it, would have confirmed the gamekeeper's suspicion that Norman and Ruari were frequently on the river, although he never actually saw them there.

So far, the evening had gone as the schoolmaster had forecast, and he was just extolling his own sagacity to his wife and some other admirers, when Prozen abruptly left the room, and returned a moment later with his violin under his chin, playing a lively Gaelic air: not only a Gaelic air, but one traditionally associated with Grimsay and looked upon by the islanders as their own. By this time, the minister had excused himself and gone and, in his absence, even the elders responded to Prozen's gesture, despite the ideological dislike of secular music with which they were indoctrinated, or which they assumed like a cloak of office, lightly but ostentatiously worn.

That was only the beginning. He played other airs, favourite airs, with a frenzied rhythm which had even the greybeards tapping their feet on the floor. It was a new experience for the violinist, used to the solitude of his own studio, or the hushed stillness of a great concert hall, between the disciplined applause which signalled his entry and the completion of each piece of music, but was in no sense part of it. Through the rhythmic drumming of the feet, the whole audience was absorbed into the song, as if they were an extension of the instrument. Foot spoke to foot, and all of them together responded to the bow. It was a celebration of the unity which he sought and, as the violinist played, the seed was sown in the mind of the composer, of the elaborate symphonic series of which only the scheme and a few small completed gems were found on his death, entitled "Sacrament on Grimsay", with the date of the 'At Home', and a quotation from Teilhard de Chardin: "At once humbled and ennobled by our discoveries, we are gradually coming to see ourselves as a part of vast and continuing processes: as though awakening from a dream, we are beginning to realise that our nobility consists in serving, like intelligent atoms, the work proceeding in the Universe."

Some of the fragments of "Sacrament on Grimsay" which have survived may actually have been played that night, in an embryonic form at least, because he went on to improvise and elaborate, so that the tunes the Grimsay crofters loved became subtly transformed: richer, more intricate, more varied. Some of the older folk regretted, indeed resented, the change: only what was familiar was acceptable. A few, but only a few, of the younger folk were also resentful: with them, their language and music were no longer an inherited habit, slowly dying out, but a cause, pursued with the brashness of crusading youth, and the narrow, abrasive exclusiveness by which every political movement inevitably diminishes its own ideal and function. The great majority, however, accepted Prozen's improvisations as an amusing experiment, something new and harmless; while a few responded wholeheartedly as they felt they were passing from a thin dawn into full daylight, or, perhaps, from the dim of twilight, with a solitary star low and faint on the horizon, into the full darkness of a frosty night, with millions of stars glittering overhead, and great swatches and swathes and shimmering curtains of aurora borealis moving across the sky with a subtle, harmonious dignity and silent grace, too swift and intricate even for a dance.

It is perhaps significant that the visual symbolism, with which those who bothered to analyse their thoughts tried to rationalise the experience they had undergone, corresponded so closely to the simile the composer himself had used, when he explained his purpose to an uncomprehending Factor.

When midnight came, Prozen, satisfied that the evening had been successful, as on the surface it had, bade them good night and announced, as the Factor had suggested, that he would keep open house for any who cared to visit the inn, so long as the stock of liquor in the cellar lasted.

The Factor had driven a hard bargain, as he always did when his employer's interests were at stake. He sold the building to Prozen, lock, stock and barrel; a phrase more appropriate than it usually is, because the unwary house-purchaser found he had enough wine and spirits on hand to last him several lifetimes and he had either to apply for a transfer of the licence and become a publican, or give away free the crates of whisky, barrels of beer and bottles of wine, which had been laid in for the coming tourist season, as well as for the local thirst.

Prozen did not grudge the cost and, being a man of moderate habits, he did not foresee the consequences. Like wasps in an over-ripe plum tree, the topers of Balmeanach, and the other Grimsay villages, buzzed in and out of the bar, night after night, relatively few in number, but vociferous in their habits: singing, arguing, fighting, vomiting. It was impossible to close the place. Some of them took up residence in the bar, sleeping where they fell, among the broken bottles, the discarded cans, the slops of beer, dripping incontinently from the tables to the floor, and mixing with the mud taken in on innumerable boots. The sleepers were as sodden without as they were within, occasionally wet with their own blood, if they slumped incautiously among the glass. And that, of course, was always good for another fight: the man who was nearest, when they wakened, was blamed for the injury.

Prozen was appalled. After the second night, he tried to resile from his bargain, but it was too late. He was besieged in his own house by a furious group of drunks, threatening to dip him in the sea, even to lynch him, if he withdrew what they now regarded as a right. Shonnie Ishbel was the ringleader. For the first time in his life, he was a man of power, the spokesman for a united and articulate group; articulate, not in their use of reasoned argument, or even coherent words, but simply because there was no mistaking their demand or their intention.

When even the privacy of his own rooms was invaded, Prozen fled. It was the only thing he could do. He returned to London until the cellar ran dry, by which time, he thought, the storm would have blown itself out, and he could return to clear up the shambles, and restore his relationship with the community.

It was during this short absence, while the orgy continued in Balmeanach, but it was still possible to dream that all would soon be back to normal, that he began to work on "Sacrament in Grimsay". There is one section of it, a raucous explosion of compelling dissonance, which has puzzled the critics, but which, to me at least, represents the threat to his vision of community, posed by intemperance in all its manifestations. There is no mistaking the Bacchanalian uproar, which forms the groundwork of the piece, but there are clamorous, high-pitched notes, rising above the general din, which can only be the unrelenting monotone of minds imprisoned in an ideology any ideology loud, arrogant, assured, and undeviating, as if seeking to drown out each other and everyone else, imposing a bleak simplicity on all the protean wealth of music, created through the ages, or still to be conceived. Behind the screech of instruments, replying to each other in an endless argument, without relating or communicating, one can hear an ominous flickering sound like flames, visualised but barely audible at first, although suggested by the music, then flaring dramatically into a roar and crackling so vivid that one can almost smell the burning, until it reaches a terrifying climax in the anguished screams of religious zealots, pronouncing doom on all who differ from them, as they create hell out of their own disordered minds, and, though they do not realise it, for their own exclusive torment.

I am tempted to argue that the holocaust as all the music critics recognised it to be was not allegorical but prophetic, but that would be stretching the evidence too far. Prozen knew of the Bacchanalian orgy, as he wrote: he had seen the beginning of it but I am not sure he really knew how accurately the other elements in the 'demoniac movement', as it came to be called, portrayed the events which were to follow in the island from which he had fled. Indeed, I think he was proceeding by intuition rather than awareness; dealing with intolerance abstractly rather than in the specific context of Grimsay. The scheme shows that the major portions of the work were to be harmonious, a celebration of the idyllic way of life although not bloodless or unreal on which he thought he had stumbled. The 'demoniac movement' was there to make the contrast; a passing threat, like a thunderstorm at sea, seen through a window from a home ashore, snarling and barking and showing its destructive power, but never really threatening the serene domestic peace within. One critic, groping towards an explanation, without knowing the background to the composition, suggested that the 'demoniac movement' represents "the irritant that makes the pearl; the disharmony, the imbalance, the flaw, the irrelevant obsession which provides the impetus for genius, like a bent bow under stress." If the composer had known what was happening in Grimsay, the dissonance would have swallowed up the harmony, the 'demoniac movement' would have been the major theme of the work, as in fact it became (although he had not planned it that way) through the accident of his premature death, before the remainder of the work was completed. To that extent the work was prophetic, but that is purely coincidental.

The sudden burst of unrestrained drunkenness reawakened all the fears, which had been momentarily stilled by the little feast of music, the ceilidh, which Prozen dramatised as the "Sacrament on Grimsay". It appeared to Maclachlan and his adherents that the foreigner was deliberately trying to debauch the young. He was not an emissary of Satan but Satan incarnate. Maclachlan denounced him night after night, at prayer meetings, as the cause of all the evils that afflicted them, real or imaginary, from the drunkenness itself to an outbreak of fowl-pest among the local poultry.

The young folk laughed at their elders' superstition, but fell into equally superstitious errors of their own. One group concerned with the integrity and purity of their language and culture regarded Prozen with a searing hatred that burned more fiercely than Maclachlan's, but which lacked the (admittedly partial and erratic) discipline which he derived from his eclectic study of Scripture. Their hatred was limitless, uncontrolled, and self-regarding, like a vortex whirling so furiously around itself that it produces a vacuum; a completely empty heart.

Another group of the young folk derided the religious and the cultural zealots alike. They began to go around at night, baaing like sheep outside the windows of anyone known to belong to either of the other factions, mocking them as blinkered fools being driven to destruction along a narrow road, because they could not see the real world around them. Their own "liberation", although they did not know it, derived from their addiction to a mythology of envy. They regarded Prozen, not as a villain, but as the victim, although in a sense also an unwitting agent of a system which must be destroyed. The devil was not in the man, but in the property he owned, the goods and chattels which distinguished him from them, and which, in the eyes of the unenlightened, raised him above them, and undoubtedly gave him power. It was they who began to preach, although not in these terms, that the curse which had fallen on them could only be lifted by a sacrificial fire.

It may well have been they who set the inn alight, but I rather doubt it. Some of Maclachlan's followers were just as ready with their matches. The Grimsay patriots, as they called themselves, had a rallying song which was full of metaphors of burning, from smoking out the foxes to sending round the fiery cross, and there were certainly among them a sufficiency of literalists, capable of mistaking the metaphors of their own propaganda for a command, or a prophecy.

It is also possible that the fire was accidental. Given even a handful of men in a drunken stupor, which lasted for weeks, wallowing in a sea of spilt alcohol, in a timber-lined building, with cigarettes as readily available as drink, the wonder is that the inn survived so long.

It is also possible, of course, that some of the drunks may have set the place on fire deliberately. As they gorged themselves on his bounty, they came to hate Prozen more irrationally than the others. Their greed and their thirst increased as the stocks diminished. They scrabbled among themselves for the vanishing whisky and, when it ran out, they called down curses on the foreigner who condemned them to drink advocaat and other unfamiliar poisons. More and more they came to see Prozen, not as the man who had treated them with unwonted liberality, but the man who deprived them when the binge was over. Before it actually struck them, they suffered the agony of withdrawal and drying out. Prozen became the devil in their delirium.

What no one knew at the time was that Prozen was in the building as it burned. If they had known, many from all the factions would have attempted to save him: humanity and courage in an emergency were never lacking. Indeed, it was in an effort to save a few drunks, whose conduct they condemned, that the two Ruaris and Norman Finlayson were lost, with four others, whom Grimsay could ill spare. It was as if the island had simultaneously lost its rudder and its keel, the two elements that gave the boat stability in a turbulent sea.

When the roof of the inn collapsed with a flurry of flame which was seen by the coastguard on the mainland, twenty miles away, who thought it was a signal of distress from a ship at sea everyone knew who was in the rescue party, clearly doomed. They also had a good idea even then, and knew for certain in the morning, who were the helpless victims they were trying to reach. It was only when a supernumerary corpse was found, some distance from the others, the few, who knew, recalled that Prozen had been seen coming off the twice-weekly steamer, barely an hour before the blaze began.

Whether he had come back for some effects, forgotten in his hurried departure, or whether he thought the orgy was over, and the time for reconciliation had begun, no one bothered to ask. They never understood his purpose sufficiently to need an explanation of his movements. Although hostility was muted by the tragedy, there were some who blamed him for the holocaust, despite the fact that he perished in it. They saw him like Samson, pulling down the pillars of the temple to his own destruction. Maclachlan interpreted it as the chastisement of God, but, when he tried to explain why the victims also included the natural leaders of the community, who had stood out against excess, his reasoning became too convoluted for anyone to follow. The Church gained in numbers, because people sought sanctuary there in a time of bewilderment, but Maclachlan lost much of his personal standing and all the supporters on whom he had previously relied.

Prozen's death made headlines in the national newspapers, but the reports did not mention that he owned the inn. Only a few of his friends had known, and they had no reason to disclose the fact. At best they knew only a fragment of the story, and what they knew seemed hardly relevant to the composer's work, or significant in relation to his death. "Famous Composer Dies in Holiday Isle he Loved" was the nearest any of the newspapers came to grappling with the tragedy.

Grimsay folded in on itself, like a sensitive plant responding to a hostile touch. The warring of the different factions ceased, on the surface at least; but this was not the unity which Prozen had seen and sought; it was the quiescence of despair; a retreat from living, which showed itself in the steady drifting away of the young, in search of jobs and a freer air, and the subsidence of the elderly into a quagmire of lifeless conformity.

With the gradual infiltration, over the years, of a group of incomers, seeking peace as Prozen had done, although they lacked his creative purpose and understanding of what it was they sought, Grimsay came alive again in a spasmodic, unco-ordinated way. There was much activity, on the surface, promoted by the incomers, but it had little relation to the deep indigenous pools of introspection below.

The local people had reasons for concealing from strangers the true story of Balmeanach Inn, so far as they knew it themselves; they tolerated with cynical indifference the 'legend' of the fairy fiddler when Grace Moir 'discovered' it; and their reluctance to pass the derelict building after nightfall gave credibility to the elaborate tale which she wove, out of her profound misunderstanding of the people she loved and sought to interpret to the outside world.

The Night of the Giant

"DID YOU EVER SEE A TALLER MAN?" asked the Bosun, pausing with a dart in his hand, ready to throw.

The Squirrel looked towards the bar. "Or a blacker!" he replied. "Even the palms of his hands are black."

"What's he drinking?"

"Guinness!"

"It would need to be – to keep his colour up."

"Up? Down!"

"Let's have him over. He's on his own," said the Bosun, some minutes later, when he had finished his throw. Handing the darts to the Squirrel, the Bosun walked over, tapped the giant on the shoulder and said, "You're pretty far from home. Come and join us in the corner."

"What are you doing here?" he asked as they sat.

"English and philosophy," said the Giant.

"Not in Totscore, you're not," said the Squirrel. "We don't know what philosophy is and we never use English – except when we're speaking to foreigners."

"In London I am doing English and philosophy," said the Giant. "Here I am studying malt whisky."

"But that's Guinness," said the Squirrel.

"Thirst!" said the Giant. "And camouflage. It matches my complexion." He gave a great laugh. "I'm the invisible man. You can't see me in the dark."

He leaned back into the shadows and practically disappeared, apart from the whites of his eyes. By this time everyone in the bar was looking and listening. Quite openly, but from a discreet distance.

"Seriously though," said the Bosun, placing a large whisky in front of his guest, "What you are doing in a dead end like Totscore?"

"Looking for a sporran," said the Giant with another great burst of laughter.

"A sporran wouldn't do you much good," said the Squirrel, eyeing his gigantic frame.

"Did you find the sporran?" asked the Bosun.

"The moths ate it!" said the Giant. "You must have big moths in Totscore. Bigger than me."

"Bigger and blacker!" said someone in the crowd.

The Giant rose to his full height. "Laugh at my size if you like," he said. "No one laughs at my colour but me!"

The tone in which he spoke sent a chill through the room.

"I'm sorry!" said the offender, and a moment later he came over with a well-filled glass which he placed before the Giant.

"Slainte!" he said.

"What's that?" demanded the Giant.

"It's a toast," said the Bosun. "It means 'Good Health!' in Gaelic. We only say it to people we respect, when we're drinking with them."

The Giant was mollified.

The Bosun and Squirrel exchanged glances. There was no need for them to speak. They were saying to each other it was a good thing Aonghas Ruadh was sober for once. If he had been in his usual truculent mood, he would not have apologised. He would probably have aggravated the offence. They could visualise the mayhem that would have resulted.

"It's a pity about the sporran," said the Bosun, anxious to know what it was all about.

"It's a pity about the moths!" said the Giant with another laugh.

"So there really is a sporran?" persisted the Bosun.

"Is?" said the Giant. "That's a good question. My professor would like that one. Is a sporran still a sporran when the moths have eaten it. The angel burned the rest. It's still all there I suppose, but some of it is moth and some of it is smoke."

"You'll have to make do with a fig leaf," said the Squirrel.

"Not in this climate," said the Giant.

"Who's the angel?" asked the Bosun, still struggling to make sense of the conversation.

"That's another good question," said the Giant. "Is or was? Is an angel still an angel when you've stopped believing in them?"

"Yes!" said the Squirrel. "Provided they believe in themselves."

"So you have got philosophers in Totscore," said the Giant. "You're wrong all the same. If they believed in themselves they wouldn't be angels. Angels never know how good they are."

"So there is, or was, a sporran, and there is, or was, or maybe an angel," said the Bosun. By profession he was a solicitor in the service of the local authority. He was called the Bosun because he was the only man in the village who had never been to sea.

"Right!" said the Giant. "I lost one, but I found the other."

"The moths didn't eat the angel?" said the Squirrel.

The Bosun was annoyed. He didn't want to be blown off course by the Squirrel's witticisms. Fortunately the Giant gave him another opening.

"Perhaps she was too tough," he said.

The Bosun pounced before the Squirrel could intervene again. "So the angel is a woman. Presumably an old woman. How do you come to be looking for a woman in Totscore?"

"I'm looking for a woman everywhere!" said the Giant expansively. The remark was without significance. Everyone who heard it knew that. A little harmless bravado. But later it was misconstrued.

When the laughter had died down the Bosun resumed his enquiry, a little apologetically. "We like to know everybody's business in Totscore," he said. "There are no strangers here. Once you've crossed the village boundary you're one of us. We want to know all about you from the day you were born to what you're going to eat for tomorrow's breakfast."

"Porridge!" said the Giant, and grinned.

"Tick off tomorrow's breakfast!" said the Bosun to the audience. The bar had become a theatre with the three protagonists seated in a corner and the others standing closely round them.

"To begin at the beginning," said the Giant, also addressing himself to the audience at large, "I am the little son of a big chief."

The audience roared.

"I am not a big man in my own country. Just average. But I don't mean it that way", said the Giant.

"My father was the chief of a very important tribe, but he had ten wives. I am the youngest child of the youngest wife. As you say in cricket, a tail-ender. A nobody."

"If I had been important I would not have met the angel and I would not be here," he added. "She was a nurse in a mission hospital. I was ill, so my father sent me there. If I had been important he would have remembered and brought me back. He forgot all about me and I was there for a very long time. The angel nursed me and taught me to speak English. Then she taught me to read and write. When at last my father remembered and called me home, she gave me a letter for him. He didn't know what it was. I had to read it to him. That impressed him. He agreed to her suggestion that I should go to school, and then to college. And here I am. The first man of my tribe to take a university degree. And all because I wasn't fit to herd my father's cows."

"Well I'm damned," said the Bosun. "The angel is my Auntie Barbara. She never seemed like an angel to me. She's the dragon of the family. This calls for a celebration."

He went to the bar to get large whiskies for his group. All the other groups also replenished their glasses. There was pandemonium until every glass was filled and paid for. Then the Bosun gave a toast, "To the Angel and the Giant. Auntie Barbara and our big friend!"

"Was she expecting you?" he asked the Giant, surprised that he hadn't heard she was to have a visitor.

"I wasn't looking for the Angel. I was looking for the sporran," said the Giant. "I had no idea who she was or where she lived. I didn't even recognise her when I saw her. But she shouted as soon as she saw me, 'It's Bobo!' That's what she called me. 'Wait till I get a chair!' I thought she was mad. I had no recollection of ever being called Bobo, but she got a chair, and stood on it so that she could put her arms round my neck and kiss me. Then she took me into the house and showed me a photo of myself in the mission hospital. A tiny little fellow all legs and ribs."

"This calls for another drink," said the Squirrel. Again there was a mad scramble round the bar. Then, imitating the Bosun, as he so often did, the Squirrel gave the toast, "Bobo and Barbara!"

"Now that you've got a nickname," he added, "you're really one of us."

"Why were you interested in my uncle's sporran?" asked the Bosun when the noise abated. "Barbara wasn't married when you knew her. My uncle's been dead for years. What, in God's name, made you travel all the way to Totscore looking for a sporran you didn't know existed?"

"It doesn't exist. Except as moth and smoke," the Giant reminded him. "But I knew it was there. I have known all my life. But that's another long story."

"Let's hear it!" came the cry from the crowd.

"My father was a soldier, before his own father died and he became Chief." said the Giant. "A soldier in your army. The British army. I saw him once in his uniform. I was proud of him. I wanted to be a soldier myself. I still want to be a soldier. I am only at the university because my country needs teachers and administrators." "Besides," he added bitterly, "my country doesn't want soldiers from my tribe." He didn't elaborate but everyone noted the change of mood.

"One day when I was a child the soldiers were parading near my home. There was a piper there. Not as big as I am now but broader. A great figure. I ran across the parade ground to get his sporran. Everyone thought I was running to my father, who was there with his own regiment. I hadn't even seen my father. I could see nothing but the sporran. It was the most important thing in my life. Perhaps it still is. I couldn't speak English then. I asked for it in my own language. I nearly pulled it off, I was so keen to get it. The piper lifted me up and carried me to a group of soldiers from my own tribe to ask them to explain why I couldn't have it. My father came forward and took charge of me. He and the piper were friends.

"When I left to come to Britain my father gave me the piper's address. He could not read it himself but he had it on a sheet of paper the piper gave him when he left the army. It was one of his treasured possessions".

The Giant took a sheet of flimsy paper from his pocket book and passed it across the table. The Bosun felt it with his fingers. Then held it to the light.

"It's a fly leaf from a Bible," he said.

"I was very lonely in London," said the Giant. "I am not a person there. In London I have no nickname!"

"One night I decided I must find someone connected with my past. Someone who could make me feel real again. I remembered the piece of paper. I wondered if the piper was still alive. Then I remembered the sporran. I might not have come for the piper, but the sporran was irresistible."

The Giant rose, towering over them. "I must be going home now, but first let me buy you a drink," he said to the small group at the table. Looking round the room, he added, "I wish I could buy you all a drink, but I am only a student. This is the first time since I left my own country – since I left my own people – I have been with friends."

"Where are you staying?" asked the Bosun. "There's no hotel in Totscore. I have the car outside. I'll run you to Tarbert. That's the nearest."

"I haven't far to go," said the Giant. Then, smiling broadly, he added, "I'm spending the night with Auntie Barbara."

It wasn't a smile of triumph, although there was triumph in it. It was the smile of a child when the gates of Paradise open unexpectedly, and life takes on a new dimension. The fact that his angel had an identity put the seal on his "homecoming".

"Look!" said the Bosun urgently. "You can't stay tonight with Barbara. Not after drinking all that whisky. She'll smell your breath before she opens the door. She's smelling it now, half a mile away. She's not opposed to drink, she's allergic to it. The least whiff drives her mad."

"I am not drunk!" said the Giant angrily, thumping the table. Everyone tensed.

"He's worse than Aonghas Ruadh," someone whispered in the crowd. "His temper's as quick as a rat trap." Fortunately the Giant did not hear.

"Look, Bobo!" said the Bosun, using his auntie's nickname for the Giant in a conciliatory way. "You're not drunk, but she is. Drunk with intolerance. The piper became an alcoholic. He died of it. Their life together was hell. She's my own aunt but I wouldn't go near her if I had a single nip within the day. You don't want to offend her or quarrel with her, now you've found her."

Bobo sat down dejected, as if he had suffered a bereavement.

"It's all right!" said the Bosun. "You'll spend the night with me. My wife will go round and tell Barbara. Tomorrow night you can stay with her. There'll be no hard feelings."

As they rose to go, the sound of pipe music was heard outside the bar. The door opened and Aonghas Ruadh came in, taking the pipes from his shoulder with a dying wail as he passed through the narrow entry.

"I'm sorry I haven't a sporran," he said to Bobo, "but at least I can give you a tune on the pipes."

Again the Bosun and the Squirrel exchanged glances. It was a miracle of peacemaking from the principal trouble-maker in Totscore. His home was a considerable distance away. He must have got a lift or borrowed a neighbour's car from the car park, to get his pipes.

Before each tune he explained its origins and associations. If the Giant had been royalty, Aonghas Ruadh could not have been more anxious to make a good impression. He was displaying an aspect of the local culture with almost ritual flamboyance.

When Aonghas had played himself out, Bobo offered to sing a song from his own country. "It's a hate song against the British. I hope you don't mind. We don't hate you now for coming to our country but for going away again. Before you came we were under the heel of the Arabs. Now we're under them again. That's why I want to be a soldier. To fight for my own people. For my freedom."

Like Aonghas Ruadh he explained each verse before he sang. It was a plaintive melody, not unlike their own. They listened intently. Absorbed in the wrongs of another country. Wrongs in which they had participated in an odd sort of way, remotely, and by inadvertence. But also wrongs which echoed their own history and identified them with the victims. At the same time they were the oppressor and the oppressed. Stirred by resentment against wrongs their own people had sustained in the past. Feeling guilt for what their country had done to others.

The final verses of the song described an uprising against the hated masters. Not the uprisings of the past which had been violently suppressed but a longed-for, millenial, triumphant revolt. As the climax approached, Bobo drew himself to his full height, brandishing a non-existent spear, which was as real as if the steel was glittering in the murky light. Then he lunged forward. Suddenly. Viciously. Striking his foe to the ground. There was cruelty and exultation in every feature, every limb, as he moved. Although his hand was empty, the crowd scattered. There was dead silence. Then a roar of applause. They were now all together celebrating the downfall of the universal tyrant. The dragon which cannot be slain because his seed lives on in the heart of the slayer. Without the seed of tyranny there would be no triumph. When the silence became embarrassing, someone turned the juke box on. Bobo began to dance. A tribal dance with sinuous movements which seemed singularly ill-suited to his massive frame but which he performed with surprising fluidity. He moved across the floor like a huge black serpent slithering and weaving and swaying on its tail.

He motioned to the by-standers to join in. The Squirrel, always ready for a bit of fun, responded immediately. For some time the others watched, fascinated by the intricacy of the dance, the surprising grace of the Giant, and the strain of concentration on the Squirrel's face as he struggled to match the steps, a half-beat behind the rhythm. The scowl changed to a smile as the steps began to repeat and he caught up with the music, although even then his movements were clumsy compared with the Giant.

At this stage some of the others began tentatively to try the steps. Gradually everyone was drawn in, writhing and wriggling, in an earnest endeavour which was almost a caricature of the original.

"I thought for a moment I had been dropped into a concrete mixer or a can of worms," said the barman afterwards. "Then, God help me, I was dancing myself."

Bobo led them out the door into the darkness, across the car park and down the village street. When they got beyond range of the juke box, he began to sing. The others took up the melody, humming or improvising words of their own.

"You're good! You're good!" said Bobo. "You'll dance it yet." Then he gave another great laugh. "It's a dance of purification. It drives the evil spirits away. We don't believe that now, but we dance it just the same. At least I don't think we believe it, though maybe we do. With our feet, if not with our heads. Especially on a night like this."

"We have a piper. Let's have a road dance!" said the Squirrel. There hadn't been a road dance in Totscore for forty years. Even if they did have one, most of them were too old to take part, by the standards of the village. But they all stirred uneasily at the sudden recollection of one of the great delights of their youth. Dancing in the open air under the stars. No electronic music. No flashing lights. No fug of smoke and stale breath. No alcohol. And the thrill of doing something illicit. Natural, free and uninhibited, but frowned on by the kirk.

Behind the wave of nostalgia, which they greeted on the surface of the mind, there was a deeper undertow. The dance they had just been engaged in was unnatural. A dance without women! A deprivation they had not been consciously aware of, although they felt it, was adding to the madness of the night.

The thought surfaced partially with the Bosun and he tried to use it for another purpose. Things had gone far enough. He wanted to stop the hysteria before it got out of hand. "We can't have a dance without women!" he said.

"Let's get women!" said the Squirrel.

Before the Bosun could remonstrate, Aonghas Ruadh and some of the others were hammering on the doors round about, or barging in without knocking. Grasping astounded housewives – other people's wives. Dragging them out of doors without explaining why. So great was their urgency it might have been a murder or a fire, an invasion from Mars, or the end of the world. But there was no panic. The men were in a mood of such exalted gaiety the women came out laughing and excited, ready to join in whatever was the ploy. A mood which many of them repudiated scornfully in the cold light of dawn.

The explanations given by their "captors" were confused in the extreme, but they knew what madness had gripped the men when Aonghas Ruadh took up his pipes and began to play an eightsome reel. Women who hadn't danced for half a century and girls who had not reached the age to begin, found themselves whirling in the darkness on the arms of men they could not see, and could not even identify by voice, because now the only sound, apart from the pipes, was the piercing, exultant, recurring scream generally described, inadequately and inaccurately, as a "hooch".

Those who found themselves in the same reel as the tangible, but invisible, giant were even more excited than the rest by the weird ululations emitted from the darkness above their heads as Bobo imitated the other men in a strange accent of his own.

At first some of the women tried to resist their involvement in the dance. From fear. Or rheumatism. From a religious abhorrence of dancing. Or a spinsterish ambivalent reaction to the unaccustomed touch of a man. Their resistance was soon overcome.

Most of them were carried away by the prevailing mood. They entered into the spirit of the night with complete abandon, although what that spirit was they had difficulty in explaining to themselves afterwards, and even greater difficulty in explaining to inquisitive neighbours from the unaffected parts of the village. It was then that Bobo's incautious remark, about looking for a woman everywhere, leaked out and was seized on by the gossips. They dissected it with clinical care, finding meanings more and more remote from the truth as their study intensified. Then they dissected with the same zeal the perversions of the original remark which their first examination had produced. And then the perversions of the perversions. It was an endless process, generating falsehood through the misguided search for truth in the distorting mirror of their own inflamed imaginations.

"My God!" said the Bosun to the Squirrel, in one of the few quiet moments when the pipes and the hooching were stilled. "There hasn't been a night like this in Scotland since Tam O'Shanter clapped eyes on the Cutty Sark."

"In Alloway's auld and haunted kirk," said Bobo, with a fair attempt at the Scots.

"What the devil do you know about it?" asked the Bosun.

"I know my Burns," said Bobo, "Just as I know my Bible. They both speak to me. Even if I don't believe them the way I used to. I know all your great poets and dramatists. They're part of my heritage just as they're part of yours. The question is how much of my own must I lose to get them. Must all my teeth be drawn so that I can have a set of false ones?"

"That's our problem in Totscore," said the Bosun.

"But you're British!" said Bobo.

"What is British?" asked the Bosun. "We're all British in Britain but we bring a great variety of cultures and experiences to being British. Our experience in Totscore has been very like your own in many ways."

"In London I see the ghosts of empire and of power," Bobo agreed. "In Totscore I see myself. In a photograph. Only it's a negative. I'm black and you're white."

"To hell with the dance," said the Bosun. He wanted to continue the discussion. "I have a net in the barn. Let's clean the river," said the Squirrel.

"Great!" said the Bosun. "A little quiet contemplation by the river is just what we need."

It was years since the Bosun had gone poaching, although at one time he had been a dedicated poacher – on principle.

When he stopped, he said he was disgusted with the way an honourable profession was being commercialised, especially by those who used poison.

"Their greed," he said, "is exactly the same as the greed of the landlords, who took the rivers from us in the first place. The fact that the law they're breaking is unjust doesn't sanctify their meanness."

His cronies looked on the change as a betrayal. He had given up because he was now an official of the local authority. He was afraid of the sack. Worse still he was becoming a snob. Growing out of his crofting background. They watched him with a more than ambivalent eye. There was fear lest the community was breaking up. Envy, because a neighbour was getting on. But there was also pride that a man of his ability and importance still lived among them, in the family home, on the family croft, and took part in most communal activities, except the one that had made the rift between them.

The Squirrel understood the Bosun's position and accepted it. But, in the exultation of the evening, he had lost his inhibitions and forgotten that he was making problems for his friend.

They moved off through the dark in a quiet philosophical mood heightened by the tension. As they went, they talked in confidential whispers about the growing pains of cultural change.

"Is it better to have a revolution – or a conquest? Chop! Chop! And it's over?" asked Bobo, "Or to succumb slowly to the pressure from an arrogant neighbour – the death of a thousand cuts? You should know. You have experienced both!"

"It's not as simple as that," said the Bosun. "We don't have a choice. Besides, those who impose the change have the same disease themselves, only they do not know it."

"Explain!" said Bobo.

"The people out there, in the middle of the stream, are moving faster than any of us but they think they're standing still. Imposing their standards on others. If they do know they're moving, they think they're leading the charge. But they're only flotsam like the rest of us."

"Metaphors are dangerous," replied Bobo. "They take you further than you want to go. But I take the point. Those of us on the edge, near the bank, can see that we're being dragged along. Those in the middle are just as helpless but they don't even know they're moving."

"Precisely!" said the Bosun. "We can tell them how the stream is setting. If only they would listen."

"That's enough big talk," said the Squirrel. "We're at the river now. We must be quiet. The enemy is listening for us."

By this time he had taken the net out of the bag and was making his way to the other side of the river, at a point where the stream was shallow and there were boulders he could step on. He knew the river so well he was able to make the crossing safely in the dark. The Bosun and Bobo remained on their own side with the other end of the net.

As they moved along, with the net stretched across the river, they quickly left the shallow bar, and moved into a rocky gorge where the water was still and deep. At the far end there was a sheer face, and a waterfall. Because of its small size and its general shape, the gorge was called "the Coffin".

The Squirrel knew there would be salmon in the Coffin. A great many had come in on the spring tide and were moving upstream. But it was a risky place to fish. Once they moved in they were trapped, if there were keepers around.

They had just reached the end of the pool and were carrying out the tricky manoeuvre of getting the two ends of the net to the same side, below the waterfall, when they heard a splash. Someone following them had dislodged a stone, as he came along the bank.

They listened for a moment.

"There's two of them," said the Squirrel. "One on each side."

"Can you swim?" asked the Bosun of Bobo urgently.

"Never mind me," said Bobo. "They won't see me. Even if they do they can't hurt me. You'll pay the fine!"

The keepers approaching cautiously through the dark could hear the voice but not the words. They were puzzled. The accent was not local. It was like nothing they had ever heard. "It must be some buggers from the south!" muttered Dan Macneil, the head gamekeeper, to himself, wishing he had taken a walking stick or something he could use in self-defence. City gangs could be dangerous.

The Bosun whispered to Bobo, "Look after yourself well. We'll be waiting for you when you get out of the gorge."

With that he stepped into the pool as quietly as he could, followed by the Squirrel. It was so deep they were able to dive below the murky surface of the water, and, with a few strong strokes, move quickly between the keepers, out of sight. It was a matter of split second timing. If they had gone too soon, the keepers could have doubled back and got them as they came ashore. If they had left it too late, they might have been intercepted, or recognised in the light of a torch. As it was they got clean away.

Silent though they had been, as far as that was possible, the noise of their movement through the water alerted the keepers.

"They're swimming for it!" shouted Macneil. "They must be locals after all."

"I'll follow them," he added, shouting to the under-keeper to carry on to the ledge and get the net.

When the under-keeper got to the ledge he felt the net under his feet. But when he bent to grasp it, it was jerked away and flopped into the water with a splash. He groped for it, but could not catch it. He shone his torch on the water but could see nothing where it should have been. "There must have been a bloody great fish in it, and he must have gone to the bottom taking the net with him," he told Macneil.

When they went back in the morning to look for the net by daylight, they found no trace of salmon or net. They knew the poachers had not been back for it, and there was no way a large net with a fish entangled in it could have cleared the ridge at the end of the Coffin, just before the waterfall.

"There must have been someone there but you let the bugger escape!" said Macneil acidly. Actually he was in no position to blame the under-keeper. Although he did not know it, Bobo had passed quite close to himself, unnoticed, with the net and two fine salmon in the net slung over his shoulder.

In the meantime the Bosun and the Squirrel had gone to earth in a hide-out they knew quite well, from which they could hear the movements of the keepers, and decide which way the chase was heading.

The Squirrel suddenly tensed. "There's someone moving close at hand!"

The Bosun looked out cautiously but could see nothing. It must be Bobo, the invisible man. "Bobo!" he called, urgently but quietly. The Giant turned towards the sound. The Bosun moved out from his cover followed by the Squirrel. They linked up with Bobo and moved off quickly towards the village.

"Dump the bloody bag!" said the Squirrel to Bobo. "I'll get it in the morning." His one anxiety now was to move quickly and protect the Bosun from the risk of capture. The air and the excitement had sobered him and his conscience was at work.

Bobo refused to give up the bag. "They're my fish," he said with a laugh. "You ran away!"

The Squirrel said no more. Voices raised in argument would have given them away. Besides, the sky was beginning to lighten in the east. They had to move quickly.

When they reached the village, all was quiet. The dancers had obviously gone to bed. The life had gone out of the party as soon as Bobo left it. He had cast a spell, even on those who had not really met him or seen him. Who knew him only as a strange sound above their heads when they were whirled unexpectedly into a dance. Some of the women claimed afterwards that the African had bewitched them. It was their only defence against prying neighbours and their own troubled minds. Be that as it may, whenever Bobo left them, the constraints and taboos of the village reasserted themselves and they slipped off guiltily into the night.

In the whole village there was only one light showing when the poachers returned. Barbara's!

"Good Lord!" said the Bosun. "I forgot to send her a message."

He turned to Bobo. "We're in trouble. She sat up all night for you!"

But Bobo was no longer there. As soon as the light was identified, he stepped over the garden gate, without stopping to open it. He was already hammering on Barbara's door.

Smelling of alcohol. As wet as if he had fallen in the river. And carrying on his shoulder a poacher's net with two illicit salmon.

"What a bloody guest for a dried out Puritan!" said the Bosun to the Squirrel, wondering how he would ever make his peace with Barbara again.

He froze as the door opened, and braced himself for the blast, keeping carefully out of sight in case his presence angered Barbara even more.

"Thank goodness you've come!" he heard her say. "I was afraid you had wandered on to the moor and got lost." There was nothing in her voice but pleasure and relief, and the warmth of welcome for her African child.

The Bosun moved quietly to the window to see what her reaction was when she discovered Bobo's condition. There were no raised voices. No hint of an argument or a quarrel. He peered through a chink in the old fashioned lace curtain. They were sitting one on each side of the fire by now, chatting amicably and drinking tea. Although he could not hear their conversation, their actions gave him a clue. His aunt was laughing at what he presumed must be an amusing account of the evening's adventures, dancing, war song, poaching and pursuit.

When Bobo paused she moved over to the bag. Took out the salmon. Held them proudly up as if admiring them. Then took them into the kitchen. Through the open kitchen door the Bosun could see her gutting the fish, as if it was the most natural thing in the world. He was prepared to swear that she was singing as she worked. Barbara the ogre! Surprised, but satisfied, he set off home.

It was time to get up rather than go to bed, but he was wet and had to change. His movements wakened Maggie. She was surprised to see him groping in the wardrobe in the half light.

"I'm looking for my Sunday suit," he said by way of explanation.

"Has someone died?" she asked anxiously.

"No!" he replied. "But I cannot wear my office suit today."

"Why?" she demanded, sensing a mystery.

"You will see when you get up," replied the Bosun, putting off the moment of explanation as long as possible.

The tactics were wrong. Maggie sat up in bed and switched on the light. She was afraid he had been in an accident. She saw the dripping suit, draped over a chair.

"You've been poaching!" she said accusingly. Swinging out of bed, she went through to the kitchen without waiting to put a dressing gown on. She looked in the deep freeze.

"What's more," she shouted to him, "There's nothing to show for the risk you took but a ruined suit. Will you never learn sense?" She was deeply worried. She knew the consequences of capture and conviction for a man in his position. She wondered whether a relapsed poacher was liable to go to extremes like a relapsed alcoholic.

"It's all right," said the Bosun. "I was just widening my experience. I made a new friend. You'll like him when you meet him. Just as I did."

"Is he wet too?" asked Maggie caustically.

"I also discovered that Auntie Barbara is human after all," he parried. Maggie was not interested. She and Barbara did not hit it off.

"Was she poaching too?" she asked, the edge in her voice still sharpening.

"No!" he said desperately. "She was singing!"

"Singing what and why?" demanded Maggie.

He was struggling to frame a suitable reply when Mary, their youngest daughter, came bouncing in with a pail in her hand. She went early every morning to a neighbour, who kept cows, to get fresh milk for the porridge.

"Were you dancing with the black man, Daddy?" she asked abruptly.

The Bosun swore quietly to himself. He knew the speed with which a rumour went round the village. He also knew how it was transformed in the process as malice, humour, envy, dullness of hearing and plain stupidity added their own perversions.

Explanation was now not only difficult; it was impossible. Suddenly he sat on a chair and laughed. Uncontrollably. His mind was running through the village, house by house, visualising the form in which the story might have taken root in each. Or rather the many forms in which it would have taken root in each. Fathers, mothers and children would all see it differently. To say nothing of grandparents and maiden aunts.

Stories of drunkenness, riot and rape would be told and listened to with glee. Even those who didn't believe the story would try to get the maximum amount of fun out of it, teasing it out as they tossed it to and fro. He thought of all the neighbours who had been involved like himself, and the women they dragged into it; trying to explain to spouses who were not there. He had a less difficult task than most of them.

Maggie was sensible. She would rag him unmercifully but she would not doubt his word. But there were others! The Bosun visualised the arguments, the disbelief, the floundering attempts at explaining the unexplainable. The confusion, suspicion, anger, perhaps violence! Nothing that TV had ever screened could equal the scenes that were taking place at that very moment in houses up and down Totscore. And it was all real.

"I think I'll open a book on it," he said at last.

Maggie was more mystified than ever. She had been whispering with Mary in a corner, and had one version of the night's events, but she knew she was still far from the truth.

"What sort of book?" she asked.

"A bookie's book!" said the Bosun. "Every punter in the place will put his shirt on some old spinster that he doesn't like. It will be a killing for the man who holds the stakes when the latest possible date has passed and no black babies have appeared!"

Afraid that Mary might ask some questions of her own, precociously indiscreet, Maggie hurried her from the room, just as Barbara came running in, breathless, without knocking.

"Have you heard the news?" she asked without preamble.

"Yes!" said Maggie. "As far as I can make out the whole village has gone mad."

"I don't mean that," said Barbara. "I mean the news on the radio. There's been a revolution."

"Revolution?" said Maggie, incredulous.

"She means in Africa," said the Bosun, guessing the truth.

"She's afraid for Bobo."

"Bobo?" said Maggie still bewildered.

"He can't go home now," said Barbara. "The tribe he belongs to will be massacred. He can't even go back to university. They'll cut his grant to force him home. They won't want an educated man, the son of a chief, roaming round the universities organising the opposition."

"What does he propose to do?" asked the Bosun.

"He hasn't heard the news yet. He's asleep. But he'll have to stay here. He has nowhere else to go."

"There's no problem there," said the Bosun. "You have the space. Mary can stay with you if you want a chaperon."

Barbara didn't react to the little joke. Clearly there was something else on her mind.

"Are you all right for money?" asked the Bosun, sensing her hesitation. He was prepared to help, as far as he could, or even, at a pinch, to organise a collection in the village.

"I'm not thinking of a week or two," said Barbara. "He may have to stay here for a very long time. I want you to get me a paper from the Crofters Commission so that I can transfer the land to Bobo. There's not much of a living in it, but it would keep him from starving. He could fish a bit as well."

"To ask a herdsman from the Sahara to become a lobster fisherman in the North Atlantic is a bit much," said the Bosun.

"Our own people had to do as much when they went to Canada during the clearances," said Barbara. "They weren't given much time to acclimatise themselves. Besides, he's a university graduate."

"That won't help him to bait a lobster creel," said the Bosun.

"Look!" he added, rising from the table. "I have to get the kids to school and myself to the office. I'll get the paper for you, but think well before you do anything rash."

"Tell Maggie about Bobo," he said, over his shoulder, as he hurried out. He felt he had got out of a difficult situation very well.

As he got into the car, he wondered how the village would react to a black man on a croft. In normal circumstances the great majority, he knew, would take it in their stride. But last night's frolic, and the rumours going around, would make it difficult. Even without that, there was bound to be some greedy neighbour who wanted Barbara's croft himself and would fight it to the bitter end. A nice little problem for the Crofters Commission!

As Maggie listened to Barbara's story, she came to realise that there was much more to her husband's aunt than she had ever suspected. Great areas of experience which never revealed themselves in a closed community, beleagured behind a ring fence of triviality. The villagers listened to the news, national and international, much as they read a story or watched a TV play.

But Barbara had a living contact with other places. A direct involvement in other people's problems.

Over the years, privately, quietly, she had kept in touch with events in Africa. Borrowed books from the library. Studied the history of the areas she had worked in. Read travellers' accounts of the peoples and places she knew. Followed current political developments, through specialist magazines she got from friends she had made in the field and with whom she still corresponded.

She was deeply interested in the new writing coming out of Africa. She seldom read a novel by a Scottish, English or American author. Fiction was trivial. A waste of time. But the African novels, she thought, were different. They dealt with the experience of people going through a rapid and difficult process of readjustment. They had parallels to the slower process which had been taking place in Totscore itself, over a long period of time. They excited, and at the same time, disturbed her, because they seemed to call into question her own part in the process, as one of the missionaries who had loosened the impacted stones of custom and superstition, setting the avalanche in motion.

She would have been upset if any of her friends had caught her reading one of the African novels. Not because it was African but because it was fiction. This part of her African studies, in particular, was pursued secretly, like the Bosun's poaching, and she got from it the same sense of being engaged in something illicit. Dangerous!

Although she did not realise it, some of her neighbours read the modern English novels she despised, secretly, in the same way, but with a very different purpose and result. The modes of thought, the language, the obsessions of a brittle, sophisticated, bewildered urban civilisation were seeping almost unnoticed into Totscore, with the result that some of the psychiatric tensions were reflected in a placid rural backwater by a process of hypochondria. In imitation of the fashionable world outside, aspiring natives of the village were deterred only by fear of their neighbours from exhibiting openly the symptoms of disorders from which they did not suffer until they acquired them by emulation.

None of this was openly on the table between Barbara and Maggie as they talked. Both of them accepted the convention that Totscore was a homogeneous, unchanging community, a fixed point in the flux of time, with the rest of the world whirling confusedly round them. They weren't even clearly conscious, as they talked, that they were observing the swirl from different standpoints. But there was a change in their relationship thereafter. Respect for each other, instead of hostility. Sympathy and understanding, although they could not say what had brought it about.

As it happened Barbara was wrong about the revolution. It presented no threat to Bobo. It was the opportunity he had been waiting for. When he wakened, he heard the news himself on a later bulletin. By the time Barbara got back to cook some lunch for him, he was gone. A brief but affectionate note conveyed his thanks and his apologies.

Her life was now emptier than it had ever been. She had glimpsed a purpose but it was snatched away from her. Disciplined by life, and faith, she went to her bedroom and prayed for the safety of her "child". Then she went back to Maggie for the comfort she would not have sought or found there in the past.

As for the villagers, Bobo's disappearance added to the general confusion. Even if the Giant had still been there, palpable and friendly, it would have been difficult to explain the events of the previous night. Now that he had disappeared, the question arose for those who had not met him: did he ever exist at all? Or was he the devil? Or was he invented as a cover up for some orgiastic madness which had overtaken all the drouths and half the kirk session to say nothing of the sombre matrons whose only outlet in the past had been the weekly prayer meeting.

Some of the women, who had been swept up into the night's events without actually seeing the Giant, began to wonder what had really happened to themselves. Had they been involved in something supernatural? Uncanny? Most shuddered at the thought. But some hoped for a recurrence. If it had happened once, why should it not happen again? Why should it not go further next time? Tremulous with fear and expectation, they waited for the coming night.

Nothing happened then, or later, but rumour was now adrift without even the semblance of an anchor to restrain it. The village humorists – and they were the majority – built the story to fantastic heights. If one black man, why not a score? If strangers from Africa, why not men from Mars? The elements common to all versions of the story were the great booze up, the tribal dance, and the seizure of the women. But everyone added trimmings to his taste. The Schoolmaster, whose one regret was that he had missed the fun, wrote a savage little poem, which included an allusion to the rape of the Sabine women. The other poems in circulation were more direct and earthier.

On the other side, of course, the censure hardened. Fire and brimstone poured from the pulpits. Sinners, unnamed but clearly pointed at, were consigned to eternal damnation for sins they had not committed. And those who wished they really had committed them were no different from those who condemned them, except that they were franker with themselves.

Nine months later it all died down. None of the consequences predicted by humour, or malice, or a sweet-sour mixture of the two, were realised. The orgy became as insubstantial as the black man himself, after he had disappeared. The incident passed into the mythology of the village. A good story, taken out occasionally, dusted over, and refurbished according to the mood of the moment.

For a short time those who had built reputations for saintliness, on their condemnation of the orgy, felt somewhat let down. The proof they had expected of their neighbours' iniquity had not materialised. But that did not undermine their self-righteousness. It reinforced it. The devil was good to his own. Even to the extent of suppressing the evidence.

Now, a quarter of a century after the event, it would be impossible to reconstruct the story by taking statements in the village. There are too many contradictions. Too much confusion. Too many axes to grind. Too many positions to defend. But if you ask the Bosun he will tell the story precisely as I have told it here. Because I am the Bosun.

But why believe me more than anyone else? I know my own truth, but I also know that it is not absolute. It is my best recollection of what took place many years ago. Filtered through my own experience. Adjusted, no doubt, without deliberate intent, to project the sort of image I want the world to have of me.

If you ask whether Bobo really existed, I can produce no evidence. Not even an entry in an hotel register. When my aunt died, I looked through her papers for Bobo's farewell message. That would have been something positive. I couldn't find it. I was so worried, I began to wonder if I was deluding myself.

I sought permission to examine the records of the local bar to see if there was a sudden surge in the takings on the night of the orgy. But what was the night of the orgy? After that lapse of time, I had no means of dating it precisely. And unless it was tied to a firm date, a peak in the takings in the bar might have half a hundred explanations.

But I do have proof. Quite apart from my belief in my own sanity. You will have to go to Africa for it. Or at least to the African news in your daily paper.

In the turmoil of a continent, where hostile tribes have been locked together, within illogical frontiers, by departing imperialists, one young man in his early twenties pleads for sanity. For a reconciliation between black and white. Not through governments, or treaties, or ideology, but by contact between ordinary people beyond the periphery of power. He has spoken frequently of a fabulous land, in the far north of Europe, which his father visited, where men and women have learned the secret of civilised living. Clearly he is Bobo's son.

If you wonder why I am so sure of his paternity I need only point to his name. Totscore! Spelt precisely as we spell it ourselves.

And there is something more, which confirms my recollection.

Once a year in the village here we take a collection for an African charity. The collection was started by Barbara, not long after Bobo's visit. Normally the villagers give generously to such a cause but, on this occasion, a considerable rump refused to give at all. Those who had taken a moral stance and were waiting for the passage of the months to reveal the sins of others! They regarded the collection as a cover-up. An attempt by Barbara, in particular, to hide her hideous lapse from grace.

The collection itself proves nothing, although the records can be traced to the year of Bobo's visit. But, even now, when the time comes to uplift it, a group of villagers refuse to help. The same people who refused to begin with! Or their descendants! If you ask them why they refuse, they cannot tell you! That lack of any logical explanation, for an uncharacteristic act of meanness, is my invincible proof, that it happened just as I have said, on the night of the Giant.

The Botcher

If you search among the nettles in the graveyard at Skigersta, on the island of Berisay, you will find a tombstone with a strange inscription. It may not be legible now, because it is some years since I saw it, and the graveyard is not well cared for. Even then, the lichen was spreading over the grey granite, obliterating the words, and I had to scrape with my penknife to make them out. If enough to whet my interest had not been clear, I would have passed the stone by. It was obviously too recent to be of historical significance. It was put there, I suppose, thirty or forty years ago. I forget the exact date, because it was the wording rather than the chronology which interested me.

Erected to the Memory
of
Doctor John Mackechnie
a so-called saint
who neglected his wife,
disowned his children,
and wasted his gifts.

Then, down at the foot, where one might expect to find a Bible text, was this line, complete with inverted commas, although I doubt whether it is a quotation from anything:

"He didn't know which end of the spoon to take his porridge with."

I had been away from Berisay for many years, and came on the stone when I was making a sentimental pilgrimage to the haunts of my youth, and also discovering those parts of the island which had been terra incognita then. I grew up in the little town of Stormhaven before the day of the motor car, and even before the day of roads, so far as many of the rural villages were concerned. When I landed on the pier at Stormhaven on that visit home, if home it can be called now I was more familiar with the centre of Liverpool and London, and the dockside area of most of the great ports of the world, than I was with villages which are now less than half an hour's journey from the house I was born in, and whose names have been familiar to me as far back as I can remember.

The eccentricity of the inscription would have aroused my curiosity in any circumstances, but my interest was sharpened by the fact that I knew John

Mackechnie well, when I was a boy at school. By that time, he was living in retirement in Stormhaven, although most of his working life had been spent in the parish of Kilmuir, which accounts for his burial in the little cemetery at Skigersta rather than in the town.

Almost every day at the interval, when we went out into the street to play football with a cork from a herring net or a tin can, because we could never, in those days, afford a football, John Mackechnie would thread his way through the scamper of boys, an old man creeping along cautiously, almost obsequiously, so as not to get in the way of our game. For that, we despised him. We would sometimes pause in our play to shout nicknames or even obscenities after him, then we would laugh and get back to the game with renewed zest.

Our white-haired headmaster, who seemed as venerable and immovable as the building in which he taught, never reprimanded us for tormenting John Mackechnie, although at times he must have heard us, and our behaviour on the streets was a favourite topic, when he addressed us solemnly in school assembly each Monday morning. This inconsistency in George Anderson's otherwise quite predictable reaction, to everything we did as boys, did not strike me at the time or, if it did, I must have shrugged it off with the assumption that he had the same opinion of John Mackechnie as we had ourselves, but it began to worry me, that day in the cemetery at Skigersta, when, suddenly, people long dead, and the events in which they had been involved, became relevant to my own experience in a fortuitous, puzzling way. The remainder of my holiday was spent in trying to find out all I could about the 'so-called saint', and his unusual memorial. In the process, I drank oceans of tea with elderly, garrulous ladies, and dispensed innumerable drams to grateful gentlemen, whose thirst was a well-kept secret from their wives. I also spent some dusty hours pouring over old school and parish records, to see whether the rigid, reticent copperplate minutes would furnish a skeleton of solid fact, sufficient to carry the wealth of gossip, speculation, invention, and honestly mistaken recollection with which my informants fleshed the story.

As I remember John Mackechnie, he always carried a large red handkerchief with white spots, with the ends knotted together to make a sort of carrier bag. "Cadger! Cadger!" we would shout, when we saw the herring tails sticking out of the back of his little bundle, or the beady herring eyes that looked as sharp in death as in life, peering at us over the edge of the handkerchief in front.

We did not feel that we had done him any injustice when we learned that he had never cadged a herring in his life. They were freely given to him by the Gaelic-speaking fishermen from the country villages, when he made his daily pilgrimage to the harbour, to see the drifters discharging their catches in the morning. I realise now that the fishermen must have seen him in a different light from us, when they pressed the herring on him but, at the time, it made him even more despicable in our eyes that the fishermen had taken a 'truas' to him.

There is no English equivalent for 'truas' that I can think of. To say that they took pity on him is inadequate. In English, 'pity' is abstract and intangible: an immanence or aura with which we surround a person, vaguely. It is true that 'truas' is also imprecise in the sense that you can say it in a different context, or a different tone of voice, to convey any of the multitude of kinds of pity of which the human heart is capable but, once the word is spoken, 'truas' is concrete, something you can almost see or handle, as real as a warm protecting blanket draped around the shoulders of a living person by a friend. I do not know whether this effect comes from the Gaelic reliance on nouns rather than verbs, or from the islanders' habit of seeing everything in terms of personal relationships rather than abstract principle, or whether the two are in some way related but, in any event, the Gaelic mode of thinking, as well as some of the Gaelic words, infiltrated the local patois of Stormhaven, enriching it greatly, although we were English-speaking town boys and thought ourselves a cut above the Gaelic-speaking crofters in the villages round about.

To us, the pity which the fishermen showed the decrepit old doctor was just as concrete as the gifts of herring through which it was expressed. The red bundle with the white spots was a badge of shame.

It was only when I began to trace the doctor's career, after I had seen the tombstone, I recollected that our 'beggar' had never been in rags. He was always decently dressed. He was always tidy. Somewhere in the background there was a frugal housewife. And, when we tormented him, he never became apprehensive or angry; he smiled quietly, as if he enjoyed our boisterous fun as much as we did ourselves, and that took the edge off our pleasure right away.

Even in his own family, I discovered, he was something of a maverick. He had few close relatives, but they were all successful business men. The closest to him, and the most important influence on his life, was his uncle Kenneth, who was a sea captain and had vessels in the China trade. Old Captain Mackechnie, unlike his nephew, knew precisely how money is made. He gathered a fortune, carrying tea and opium from Shanghai to any port in the world which was open to receive a cargo. He drove his crews hard, and his ships harder. It was said that on one occasion, when he arrived at Liverpool, his vessel was so strained by the storms he had battled through, Lloyds would not insure either ship or cargo, for the onward voyage to Baltimore, so he took out some sort of policy with a bucket-shop company, which has long since vanished, slipped out of harbour under cover of darkness, and crossed the Atlantic in mid-winter, with the crew at the pumps continuously, day and night.

It was a mad escapade, but his men went with him willingly: he treated them as equals, although he kept a firm command; he was generous in his settlements; and his skill, his courage and his success, were proverbial in the ports he frequented.

It must have been about the time of that voyage to Baltimore his brother-in-law wrote to him about John, who was then a youngster. The schoolmaster thought highly of John's ability and wanted to send him to college: would the captain help his sister's son?

Captain Kenneth, who spent with the same panache as he earned, wrote back, "Send the lad to college. I'll give him £50 a year as long as he's there." Fifty pounds a year was riches indeed for a lad from Berisay a century ago, and, before he left Aberdeen, John had taken degrees in Arts, Medicine and Divinity. Cynics in Stormhaven thought he was determined to cling to his £50 as long as he could. "It's more than he could earn at anything he set his hand to," they said, with some truth, hinting that he would still be a student, when he was as old as Methuselah, unless his uncle shut the tap. But those who knew him better realised that he took to learning the way others take to drink. Like a horse in a park, he would eat and play, as long as the grass was green, because it was his nature to do so, never pausing to think that his real function in life was pulling a farmer's cart.

Although they criticised him, or made fun of him, his acquaintances in Stormhaven were greatly impressed by the degrees he acquired and the prizes he won. Sooner or later, they believed, a genius like that must make his mark in life; but the old captain said, a little dryly, "I made a promise and I'll stick to it, but I would sooner see the lad a decent shoemaker than a jack of all trades."

John Mackechnie tried his hand at teaching first, in the Free Church School at Stormhaven, where he had been a pupil. On his first day, when he lifted the lid of the teacher's desk to get the register, half a dozen field mice jumped out and went scurrying round the classroom. The girls screamed and stood on the benches. The boys, who were much more numerous, chased the mice hither and thither, tripping over each other, upsetting desks, shouting instructions, pushing the teacher this way and that, and generally tearing the place apart. One big chap pretended to catch a mouse with a rugby tackle, missed his aim, and brought the master tumbling to the floor instead. The big chap helped the master to his feet, ostentatiously dusted him down, to remove the stains of battle, apologised for his clumsiness, and took his seat. That was the signal for the class to settle down and wait for events, as if they were the best behaved pupils in the universe, but now and then a fresh commotion would break out, as one of the boys reached forward under the desks with an outstretched foot to touch a girl's leg and set her screaming that a mouse had got under her skirt. Next day there were homing pigeons in the teacher's desk, and on the third day an angry and dishevelled hen. The teachers in neighbouring rooms, unable to work through the uproar, complained to the headmaster, a prim little martinet with a black beard, pince nez, and an acid wit. His name came as a shock when I discovered it. George Anderson had been there in fact before the building, in which I had been taught, but it was difficult to reconcile the account I was given of a stern, unimaginative, rigid, black-bearded disciplinarian with the mellow, white-haired, father-figure of my own schooldays. But, however his appearance, and perhaps even his personality, might have changed, George Anderson at all times was a realist, liberal-minded and possibly in advance of his day, but never getting too far out of touch with the authorities on whom his bread and butter depended. He knew precisely how a school must be run, to get as many pupils as possible through their examinations on a set curriculum and that, he also knew, was the only thing about a school that could be measured, and judged (apart from attendances), not only by the leaden shopkeepers and hidebound ministers on the committee to which he was accountable, but even by his senior colleagues in the Inspectorate.

"You must control your pupils or look for another post," he said to his new recruit, or something pretty close to it, and the struggling newcomer pled for time.

"No one ever controlled a class who did not master them the first day," Anderson continued. "I doubt you've lost the battle."

"There is no battle," pled John. "We are all friends. It's the only basis for true education."

"There's only one way to deal with an unbroken colt, and you've got a classroom full of them. If you had a little backbone, there might be a battle and that at least would be a beginning."

There was no battle. It was not in John Mackechnie's nature to fight, at least not to fight in the overt aggressive way that the world admires. But equally it was not in his nature to give up. When the boys ran temporarily out of ideas (or livestock) they listened attentively enough, for he taught them history, geography, literature, current affairs, and even mathematics, not as separate disciplines, or lessons to be learned by rote, but as a lively adventure in which they were themselves involved, in which the movements of the vessels they saw each day in Stormhaven harbour were incidents, as were the voyages of which their fathers and their uncles spoke. Even some of the simple articles in domestic use in their homes became exhibits and clues in the story they sought to unravel.

When he asked them each to bring something to school from a foreign country, and tell him about it, the classroom looked like a pawn shop or a displenishing sale, at some eccentric undiscriminating museum. There were trinket boxes made with porcupine quills; wooden coggies or bowls from the Baltic ports, with Russian designs in black and red; huge sea shells which were passed from hand to hand so that every pupil could hear for himself the roar of the breakers on distant fabled shores; dusty old sextants with which he taught the boys to read the sun; beads of all sizes, shapes and colours with which the girls, and indeed some of the boys, adorned themselves and pranced in front of a strangely decorated mirror made in Birmingham but picked up by an island seaman in the South Sea Islands, where he thought it belonged; there were silks from China, porcelain from Japan, coins with inscriptions in languages known and unknown, which provoked endless arguments as to their provenance and their value; quaint knives and tools of Eastern manufacture; pictures made from butterfly wings; pieces of coral, even a quantity of Archangel tar which quickly found its way into half the inkwells in the class; moccasins with shiny beads from Baffin Bay, a cat o' nine tails which the boy who brought it swore had his father's blood congealed on the thongs, and strange carved figures from Easter Island which the girls wrapped up in their handkerchiefs and pretended to nurse.

And so it progressed for a period. At times there was uproar in the class and at times a hush, as they listened entranced to a story or an explanation. It is difficult to know which worried the schoolmaster more, the noise or the calm. When the latter occurred, he stood outside the door striving to find the cause, and heard nothing from the teacher remotely related to the curriculum set for the class.

"I've passed more examinations than anyone in the school, but it hasn't made me a good teacher or a good man," said John Mackechnie when Anderson remonstrated with him.

"Yes," retorted the head, "and if there had been a degree in idiocy you would have taken that as well – with honours."

He hated his new assistant, not so much because of the threat to general discipline in the school, although that was real, and he was determined not to tolerate it, but because Mackechnie's ideas on education came close to his own. His integrity as a teacher was under attack as well as his authority: that was what really hurt. Not that the attack was deliberate. Mackechnie had drifted into the situation because of his weakness, but he was using teaching methods which Anderson believed in, although he knew neither the School Board nor the pupils nor the curriculum were ready. He went as far as he could in the same direction, but prudently: he never left the buoyed channel, and he felt frustrated and humiliated when he saw the less experienced man making boldly for the open sea, even although he knew that inevitably he must come to shipwreck.

His hatred was intensified by the knowledge that, to protect his own position, he must report his problem to the school managers before they learned of it by common gossip. He had no doubt that was the correct thing to do, and no hesitation in doing it, for he had the political instinct for survival, which is essential to any short-term achievement in life, but the element of treachery to his own ideals, no less than to a colleague, irked and irritated like a stone in his shoe. John Mackechnie had no right to place him in that position!

The managers' meeting went well enough. Before the headmaster was halfway through his report, the chairman interrupted him with an emphatic, "He'll have to go. The sooner the better."

Frank Mitchell, the committee chairman, was a fish curer, greatly respected for his business acumen. He could look at a half-basket of herring taken as a sample from a catch of a hundred crans, and decide in a flash how much he could afford to pay, having regard to the catches already in port, the prospects of more to come, the number of gutting women available, and the demand for kippers in Billingsgate or cured herring in the Baltic ports. His flair for the price of fish was as precise and accurate as the instinct of the swallow for building a nest but, like the swallow, he was imprisoned in his own skill. Over the rest of life he was as short-sighted as a mole, as dogmatic and belligerent as a seagull.

Some members of the committee had misgivings because Mackechnie was a local man, with relatives who might be expected to exert pressure on his behalf, but they were more intimidated by the presence of Frank Mitchell at the head of the table than the prospect of meeting a Mackechnie faction in the street later on. They held their peace, relying on their ability to place the blame on someone else, when the outside pressure began.

That night at supper, Anderson was able to tell his sister Jess, who kept house for him, "The only one who spoke up for him was Noble, the solicitor, and no one pays much attention to the maunderings of that old drouth."

"Drouth or not," said Jess, "he has the sharpest brain in Stormhaven and he knows quality when he sees it. He would never have been stranded in a place like this but for his weakness. If he thought John Mackechnie worth fighting for, it means something."

Anderson was surprised. Jess shared his views on most things and, even when she disagreed, she concealed the fact out of respect for the schoolmaster's position – and his self-esteem. Besides, she was an ardent worker in the Temperance movement and despised Noble as a weakling and an evil influence on the young.

"I don't know how I will break it to him," said Anderson, ignoring his sister's comment as he pursued his own problem. "It will be a shock to his pride, but surgery is necessary for the sake of the school."

"You won't find him difficult, George," said his sister. "In fact, he's already decided to leave. A man with his qualifications is wasting his time in a school like this."

"Has he made you his confidante?" asked Anderson with some acerbity. He disliked the implication in his sister's remark that his subordinate was better equipped academically than he was.

"I would rather say I persuaded him to it," said Jess.

"I wish you wouldn't interfere in my affairs," said Anderson sharply. "In this instance it certainly relieves me of an unpleasant responsibility, but it may not always work like that."

"George, my dear," said Jess, sitting on the arm of her brother's chair, and putting her arm around him affectionately, "how blind can you be? I know the school is the beginning and end of life for you, but not for me. I am not interfering in your business but in my own. John and I are to be married."

Anderson's diary is a discreet little book; even although it was written for no-one's eye but his own, it always presents the public image of the schoolmaster, never his inner and wayward thoughts. It is almost as colourless as the official minutes, but even so one can sense the shock and anger he felt, when his sister told him her secret.

How ludicrous he would look, walking down the aisle, in a crowded church, to give his sister in marriage, to a man he had just declared in public was not fit to be a junior teacher in his school. How would he receive him in his home, now that he had thrown him on the street? If only she had told him before the meeting, before he had shown his hand!

And what about his own domestic arrangements? Jess had a mind as good as his own and shared his interests, he could talk to her about the school in the evenings, and buttress his own uncertainties with her ready sympathy and assent. The idea of living with a housekeeper was intolerable, and of marriage, worse. Where would he find a suitable wife, in a dull provincial backwater like Stormhaven? He thought of all the dismal tabbies he met at church socials, whose minds never rose above the sandwiches and tea. They sometimes came to hear him lecture, and the fatuity of their praise made him scream, silently, but with a raw anguish.

So far he had not spoken, but Jess understood something at least of what was passing in his mind. "George," she said solemnly. "don't imagine that you are trying to raise this community to your own intellectual level. A thought like that would flatter you and degrade you at the same time. You're merely providing stepping stones, or a ladder. Some of these youngsters will scramble over your back to heights you could never attain yourself. That's the glory of your calling."

"What's this got to do with you marrying that man?" growled her brother.

"Just this," she said lightly. "you must wait a year or two, and then you can marry one of your old pupils. I can think of quite a few who could be far more to you than ever I can be, intellectually, as well as in other ways, once they mature."

The schoolmaster rose without a word and left the room. For weeks he scarcely acknowledged his sister's presence, when they met at mealtimes, and he never spoke to her unless he had to. He had been blind to her growing affection for John Mackechnie, although it was in the schoolhouse they had first met, before he discovered his protege's shortcomings. She had been equally unaware of the torments her bachelor brother suffered, day by day, in a classroom of nubile girls. The suggestion that he might let himself fall in love with one of them, then or even thereafter, threatened the defences he so painstakingly maintained. And yet, a few years later, he did just as his sister had foreseen. There is no evidence that he had any special affection for Marion Ross, while she was a pupil in the school, but she came back after her training as a teacher, and in a very short time she was installed in the schoolhouse. She made him a perfect wife, bridging the gap between him and the bilingual community, in which he had settled to pursue his life's work, filling out and mellowing his personality by the gentle loving irony with which she sustained the pretence of being still the deferential pupil, sitting at her master's feet, although more frequently, in the real business of living, he could learn from her.

Jess and John Mackechnie, for their part, were quietly married in Edinburgh in the presence of a few friends. She did not invite her brother, or even tell him that the date had been fixed, but after her marriage she wrote him a letter which survives.

"It hurt to get married without the presence of the one person, apart from my husband, for whom I really care, but it would have been an embarrassment for all of us had you been there, or had you declined to come. Not that I impute any fault to you, or to John, or even to myself, in this miserable business. We were all victims of the circumstances which led John into a position for which he was not fitted, but if he had not made that mistake, I would not have met him, and that would have been a great loss to me. There is a special providence even in the fall of a sparrow, and I believe John is being called by his Lord to a service in which I am honoured to be his humble helpmate."

"He is shortly to be ordained as a minister and his gifts, I am certain, are much more suited to the pulpit than the hurly-burly of the classroom. And how the Church needs men of his eloquence, wisdom and understanding! It is a paradox of God that a man who fails in small things may succeed in great and John, who was unable to fill a junior post, in a little school, in his native parish, will shine in the pulpit of a great city church, where he can preach to the highest in the land. He is modest and unsure of himself, but we have been given a Divine injunction that our light must not be hid beneath a bushel."

It was in that bright hope that Jess's marriage began, and it is to her credit that she never lost faith in her husband, or failed to sustain him, in the dreary years that followed.

The truth is that John Mackechnie preached in city churches and country parishes, to crofters in the wilds of Ross-shire, to shepherds in the Border hills, to miners in Lanarkshire and fishermen along the Moray Firth, but he never found a congregation prepared to give him a call.

It is difficult for us to understand today how such a situation could have arisen, but Scotland, at the end of the last century, was a very different country from the one we know today, and the Church of Scotland was a very different institution. There was no scarcity of aspirants for the ministry and wherever John Mackechnie preached someone else was preferred.

City congregations were prepared to tolerate his liberalism, and felt flattered by the great philosophic sweep of his argument, even though they could not follow it, but they were irritated by his accent, and his illustrations, drawn from the petty lives of the shoemakers, carpenters, fishermen and sailors he knew in his native town. "Can any good thing come out of

Nazareth?" they asked, although they did not use these words, and did not realise that the periphrastic words they did use carried the same arrogant and ignorant connotation.

The country folk were suspicious of his academic record and his scholarship, even before they heard him preach.

Sometimes they concluded "He's nae for the likes o' us", and did not even ask him to preach a trial sermon. When he did receive an invitation, they warmed to him as a man, but missed the smell of smoke and brimstone to which they were accustomed. A preacher, who did not shake the sinners over hell, gave very little satisfaction to those who thought they were saved.

Behind these superficial, but still compelling, reasons for his lack of success there was something deeper: his liberalism was not permissive; he was not the forerunner of the ministers of the present day, whose yoke is easy and whose burden is light, in a very different sense from that intended by Scripture; he preached love, not tolerance, and the sacrifices, which he saw that love demanded, terrified his hearers, whose primary concern was with their own personal property and, after that, the property of the institutions they supported.

In the end he persuaded no one but himself. "Here I am," he said one night to Jess, "pouring out my soul, like a thrush, in a song of love and sacrifice and service. But why am I doing it? So that I can get a quiet country parish where I still have plenty of time to bury my head in books or, better still, a fashionable city charge where I can wax fat and lazy on the hospitality of rich parishioners. My own life is a mockery of everything I preach."

Jess smiled a wry, ironic smile. Life since their marriage had been insecure and penurious. John had earned nothing but the meagre fees from short intermittent periods of employment in a vacancy here and there, a vacancy which always terminated in a call to a man in every way his inferior. She could think of no greater sacrifice than he was already making, but she held her peace. She knew that they could not continue as they were going and, however mistaken the motives which made her husband seek a change, she was glad that their problem was at last out in the open.

They discussed the matter off and on for weeks without reaching a decision. Sometimes John himself would bring it up in a mood of self-criticism and despair. Sometimes Jess would broach it gently in an effort to edge him to some practical conclusion. In the event, his mind was made up by his uncle's death. Captain Kenneth had a sizeable fortune, and, for want of nearer relatives, he left it all to John.

"Now at last I can do precisely what I want," he told his wife, when he returned from the funeral with the news of his uncle's will. "I am going to build a hospital in Stormhaven and work as a doctor among the poor."

Jess was shocked by his perversity. She could not see him as a doctor. He was not strong enough physically for the rigours of an island practice, and he lacked the decisiveness that a doctor needs. Besides, his great gifts of intellect and language would be wasted. She reminded him that, although he had never got a call, in every congregation where he preached there was a strong minority in his favour. If he wrote, instead of preaching, his message would reach sufficient numbers to give it significance. His might be the very voice the nation needed to hear. His uncle's money, if he kept it, would give him the opportunity to evangelise in the way he was best fitted for.

"I know you are concerned about the home and the children," he said, in reply to all her arguments. "But this inheritance is not ours. It has been given us for a purpose. I would never have a moment's peace, if I were to live in comfort on money, which my uncle acquired in ways which I would probably disapprove of, if I knew the truth."

She reminded him that it was his uncle's money which had sent him to college. But for that, he would probably be a fisherman or a cooper, working with his hands in Stormhaven. "Not", she added, "that you would have been a great success as either."

It was the only time she ever said anything to him intended to hurt, but she was fighting for her children.

John smiled. "I would have been a botcher, wouldn't I?" he said, and that was all.

She felt relieved that she had not succeeded in hurting him, but frustrated because she had failed to move him from his purpose. With a good grace she made the best of things, rearing her family on his meagre earnings as a country doctor, while the inheritance was conveyed to trustees for the Stormhaven hospital, in a manner which led them to think that it had come to them directly, under the Captain's will.

When the news got around in Stormhaven, people wondered what had moved the old man to make such an unexpected decision on his deathbed.

Just how meagre John Mackechnie's earnings as a doctor were, in the years that followed, was apparent when I thumbed through his books of account: an interminable record of debts accrued but never collected. Many of his poorer patients obviously did their best to pay him by a form of barter. There are records of gifts of a fowl, a dozen eggs, a salmon (poached, no doubt), a haunch of venison, or even a string of haddocks. There was no relationship between the debts and the gifts, and quite large bills were marked "discharged by the gift of a fowl" or "paid by a skirt-length of tweed." A scribbled note on one page revealed that a widow whose only child he had nursed through a fever came to the surgery once a week for several years bringing gifts, sometimes amounting to no more than a single egg. He had obviously tried to dissuade her without success, and the record concluded with the words in the doctor's handwriting, "grossly overpaid", although whatever inflated value I put on the gifts could not approach the charge (the very modest charge) which stood against the widow's name.

Against many of the larger debts stood the names of people I had known in my youth as the would-be aristocrats of Stormhaven, people whose families had lacked for nothing, and who lived not only well, but ostentatiously. The largest debt of all stood against the name of Frank Mitchell. Not a penny was recorded as having been paid against it, and the amount was so much greater than any other in the book I made enquiries to discover how it came about.

"I think it was the cholera," one old man told me, whose father had been a close friend of Mitchell's. Others said it was typhus, or small-pox, which had broken out in the Mitchell household. The existence of some unusual infection was not surprising. Mitchell's work as a fish-curer, and as vice consul for a number of foreign powers, brought him in touch with many seamen, visiting Stormhaven for trading purposes or under stress of weather.

Whatever the illness, there is a tradition among the old folk that Mackechnie was called in, although he was not the family doctor, and acted with the decisiveness which characterised his work in the medical field, in spite of his wife's forebodings. He isolated the house completely, arranged for massive quantities of disinfectant to be poured daily down the drains, took up residence in the house himself, nursed the family and attended to their domestic wants. He arranged for his own children to purchase what groceries and medicines were required, leaving them at an agreed spot so that there was no contact whatever between the members of the stricken family and the rest of the community. All but one of the Mitchell family recovered and the disease did not spread.

It is difficult to understand why a man like Mitchell, who received so great a service, should be reluctant to pay for it, and why the doctor, who rendered the service, should have refrained from pursuing his claim against a wealthy client, if need be, through the courts. One can be cynical and say that Mitchell's greed was greater than his pride, and Mackechnie's pride was greater than his greed. My own belief is that Mackechnie was so immersed in his work he was almost unaware of the debts owing to him and the remedies available, if they were not paid, while Mitchell, who seems to have been in commercial terms a thoroughly honest man, may have unconsciously suppressed the recollection of the debt because it hurt him to acknowledge that he owed an obligation, which money could never discharge, to a man on whom he had inflicted great injury at the outset of his career.

Whether that is so or not, one thing seems clear: Mackechnie was quite unaware of the effect his lack of mercenary instincts had on his wife and family. Fortunately, by the time his health broke down, and I became aware of him, roaming the town with a hanky full of herrings, his son and daughter were both contributing to their mother's upkeep. It was his son who, after his death, and against the wishes of his mother and sister, erected the granite slab, with its savage memorial, to a man whom the crofters and fishermen he laboured among remember as a saint.

The Kilmanoevaig Mummy

IT WAS THE SCHOOLMASTER who christened them “the Weathermen”. It was an analogy the villagers would never have thought of, and for the most part did not understand, but the name stuck.

“You know,” he said in explanation, “they’re like one of these little cottages you used to get, with two figures. When it was wet, one came out. When it was dry, the other came out. There was always one of them out, but they were never out together.”

The villagers were still baffled. They had never seen a toy weather house. But they understood the point the Schoolmaster was making.

Robertson Mor had his home at one end of the straggling line of buildings, enclosed by a high white wall, which comprised Kilmanoevaig distillery. Robertson Beag had his home at the other. There was no relationship between them: at least no relationship close enough to trace if you were not an expert on genealogy. The link between them, apart from the name, was that they were both in the knitted goods trade. They travelled regularly to England, and even abroad, looking for markets for the hairy Kilmanoevaig sweaters, made from local wool, which were sometimes high fashion, and sometimes unsaleable. The point of the Schoolmaster’s crack was that never by any chance did they go on their travels at the same time.

The villagers concluded that they were torn between the desire to get orders, and the desire to get knitters to fulfil the orders they already had. When one was in London or New York, providing for the future, the other was at home, nobbling his rival’s knitters to make sure of the present.

Although they could conduct themselves with ease in the buyer’s office of a Fifth Avenue store, or even in the little back room of a Carnaby Street boutique, they were still an integral part of the Kilmanoevaig community. It would be wrong to say that they darted in and out of the village like chameleons taking the colour of each new background as they went. There was nothing darting about their movements, or their slow West Highland drawl, and they took no colour from their changing background. Their secret was not camouflage but integrity. They were themselves wherever they went, and accepted everyone they met without surprise, or criticism, or prejudice, on his own terms. In fact the secret of their adaptability was that they did not adapt.

They were both prosperous by Kilmanoevaig standards, but not excessively so, at least until Robertson Mor, by an odd mischance, had a formidable win on the football pools.

"Now," said Mary, his wife, "we can rebuild the house as it ought to be. We have a magnificent site."

The villagers always believed that she was the real manager of Robertson Mor's business. That he was merely a salesman carrying out her orders. They over-estimated the momentum of her bustling talk and movements. They under-estimated his inertia. His calculated and deliberate inertia.

"No, my dear!" he said. "We don't build anything. We have a problem on our hands."

He had no need to explain. She knew he was anxious not to disturb the delicate equilibrium between himself and his neighbours. The villagers enjoyed the rivalry between the two Robertson families, contained within a pretence of friendship. And yet not quite a pretence. The rivalry was there, concealed, or partially concealed, by a thin skin of superficial, almost ostentatious, friendship. It was the interplay at that level the villagers watched with glee. But below, at the heart of their relationship, beneath the rivalry, was a deep and genuine sense of belonging to the same community. An acceptance of each other, which in some ways surpassed friendship. The relationship was not a simple one, but an elaborate mechanism of adjustment, made for the most part spontaneously and without conscious thought, which worked very sweetly, as long as the balance between the parts was not too violently disturbed.

That was one element in his caution, but there was another. Gambling on the football pools was forbidden by the church to which he and his wife both belonged. Robertson Mor was no hypocrite. He made no pretence of being better than he was, and he imposed no standards on other people which he did not apply to himself. He would have been delighted to hear that one of his neighbours, preferably one of his poorer neighbours, had come up on the pools, and would have defended him, as far as he could, from the wrath of the kirk session. But, if he were forced to defy the kirk session himself, in public, he would have to sever his connection with the church, and possibly with the village. He did not want to provoke an intolerance he would feel himself obliged to resist.

"They don't need to know where it came from," said Mary. "After all, you're doing well in the business. How is anyone to know you haven't done that little bit better."

"Everyone knows how many knitters I employ. Robertson Beag is there as a check on me. They can see precisely how well I'm loaded, just as surely as if I were a ship riding in the harbour, with a Plimsoll mark along the water line."

"You mean you are going to put it in the bank, and leave it there, gathering interest which we cannot use? I would sooner see it gathering green mould. It would be too tantalising for words."

"All I am suggesting is caution," he replied. "A sudden display would have the villagers talking. We won't go into top gear right away. We'll accelerate slowly."

However delicate the manoeuvre, a change of gear does not go unnoticed in a closed community. Robertson Mor soon found himself making the very explanations he had tried to avoid. Sometimes he murmured vaguely about a tip on the Stock Exchange, or his luck with the Premium Bonds, which, although also condemned, were less offensive than the pools. Occasionally he spoke of his good fortune in meeting up with a buyer, who had more money than sense and didn't know the price of knitted goods.

"It's funny I never came across a sucker like that, although I cover the same beat," was Robertson Beag's dry comment, when the last proposition was put to him by the Schoolmaster, whose hard little envious mind was drilling into the problem like a gimlet – a tool which has its uses in association with others, but, by itself, produces nothing but holes and sawdust.

Unlike the Schoolmaster, Robertson Beag was not envious. He had enough for his own needs. He was certain his rival had not out-smarted him, and a stroke of luck on the Stock Exchange or Premium Bonds was no skin off his nose. His wife, Janet, was not so easily satisfied. She was no more envious than he was, but she was inquisitive. She could not understand her husband's cautionary, "Look Janet! Those who ask too many questions about other people may find themselves answering awkward questions about their own affairs."

Her reply was explosive. "We have nothing to hide!"

"More's the pity!" he replied with a laugh. "If people get into the habit of asking questions it's not what they find out but what they suspect, or invent, that becomes important. Asking questions melts the glue!"

"What glue?" she demanded, exasperated by an allusion she could not understand.

"The glue that binds us together in a reasonably contented community," he replied. "No one knows what it's made of, or how it works, but, by God, it's easily destroyed when the rats get nibbling at it."

"I still want to know how they can afford to run that car?" said Janet, looking out the end pane of their big bow window, from which she could see a brand new Mercedes parked at Robertson Mor's gate.

"They can't!" said Robertson Beag. "Unless he's living on an over-draft. When a man with his size of business begins spending like that he's having a last fling because he knows he's broke." He had no real fear of his rival's stability. He knew that Robertson Mor was the sharper businessman of the two, but he wanted to give his wife an explanation that would keep her happy because it held out the prospect of further drama to come, with the crash.

Six months later there was still no sign of a crash and she returned to the problem. It was the time of year when the whole village, including the two Robertson families, moved out to cut the peats, responding to the season as the birds and the field mice do, rather than making a conscious decision, in response to the calendar or the thermometer. It was a chore, but it was also a ritual. Even those, like the two Robertsons, who had oil-fired central heating, still cut peats to burn in a ceremonial fireplace. In fact Mary had insisted, as one of the changes cautiously introduced into her household, that they should have an open hearth in the middle of the largest room, round which her guests could sit, as if in an old thatched house, reviving the ceilidh tradition, with a soot-caked hook (or slabhraidh) on which she could hang a kettle to make tea, or heat the water for a goodnight toddy before they ventured into the winter storms. Instead of the hole in the roof which served to let the smoke away in the old black house, she had a canopy of burnished copper, suspended from the roof tree, well above eye level, with an extractor fan concealed within it, to make sure that none of the smoke strayed into the room, giving her expensive draperies the characteristic smell without which the old folk, who remembered the black houses she was imitating, were not prepared to accept her ceilidh room as authentic.

The ostentation of this aped simplicity was very much in Janet's mind as she and her husband joined the pilgrimage to the peat banks. The new room had just been completed and was the principal subject of speculation and gossip. As if underlining the point for her, in the ill-formed lay-by on the rough peat road, amid all the cheap and ancient cars, the creels and the wheel-barrows, Robertson Mor's Mercedes shone out like a neon sign advertising the owner's wealth.

"I wonder has he a gold-plated tarasgair?" asked Janet peevishly, pointing to the rusty peat spade her husband was taking from the car boot. With a wave she directed his attention to the bank where the Robertson Mors were busy. Similar conversations were taking place all round about, and as envy is both infectious and self-perpetuating, the topic might have kept them going for the rest of the summer, if their thoughts had not been directed into another channel by a sudden shriek from Mary.

"God!" said the Schoolmaster, "You would think she had never seen a mouse before. Her father's shop was hotching with them. You often bought one with a bag of meal."

As soon as he spoke, he knew it was not a mouse. Robertson Mor was on his knees in the bog, looking at something. It was clearly something immobile. He stood up quickly. Spoke briefly to his wife. Then the two of them hurried across the moor to the car. By this time the villagers from all the peat banks round about were converging on the spot the Robertsons had left to see what it was that had so disturbed them.

Thrusting up from the chocolate brown mud, where Robertson Mor had just cut a peat, they saw, when they got there, an unmistakeable human foot.

The Schoolmaster quickly filled his cap with water from a stagnant pool and poured it over the protruding object to wash away the peat with which it was coated.

"I want to see if there is flesh on it or is it a skeleton," he said, dropping on his knees as Robertson Mor had done a few minutes earlier. Even after several applications of water, with which he now had many helpers, it was not easy to see precisely what was there, but eventually he stood up and said, "It's a body, not a skeleton. But it's been there a long, long time. The skin is all withered and shrunken, but the peat has preserved it."

Some of the younger men got their spades, as if to dig the body out. Robertson Beag restrained them. "I had a word with him in passing," he said. "He's gone to phone the police. We must leave things as they are until they come."

The crowd divided into little groups in animated conversation. Then, when they saw that nothing further was likely to happen for some time, they returned to their own peat banks and their humdrum task, lifting an eye now and then towards the main road to catch the arrival of the police, or towards Robertson Mor's peat bank to speculate on the origin and significance of the body buried there.

There was great resentment when the police did arrive, because they immediately screened the "locus" off.

"They're putting up the shutters," growled the Schoolmaster. "Not even the dead belong to us now!"

The older folk drifted home disgruntled, feeling they had been cheated out of a drama which properly belonged to them. The younger folk hung around the screens, peeping and peering, and getting in the way of the police.

Eventually the body was wrapped in a sheet and carried away, leaving the villagers with nothing to look at but a hole in the ground. Although there was plenty of speculation, and even confident assertion, they had to wait for the weekend, and the arrival of the "local" newspaper, printed in a distant town, before they got the facts, or some of the facts, about something which had taken place on their own doorstep. A body which was part of village history, although it had lain unnoticed beneath the peat for hundreds of years, had vanished for good into a distant museum where few of them saw it. Their share of the discovery had been a fleeting glimpse of a blackened toe.

"It's precisely as I said," announced the Schoolmaster over his Saturday breakfast, with the local paper propped up before him. "The body is that of a man of the 18th century. The peat has preserved the clothes as well as the body. Everything is intact although dyed brown by the peat."

"What age was he?" asked his wife.

"I said a man, not a horse! You can't tell his age from his teeth."

"What was he doing, dead in a bog?"

"Lying very still, as dead men do!" said the Schoolmaster sarcastically.

"That's not funny," said Margaret. "You know quite well what I mean."

"You would be dead yourself if you had a hole in the back of your head," said the Schoolmaster. "You're that busy with stupid questions you don't give me time to tell you what the paper says. It looks as if he had been murdered by a blow."

"I wonder who did it?"

"You're not the only one!" snorted the schoolmaster. "This paper is going to the dogs. The report is headed 'Where's Agatha?"

"Who's Agatha?" asked Margaret.

"For God's sake, woman! Agatha Christie! The woman who writes detective stories."

"But she's dead!"

"I know she's dead. They wonder what she would have made of it if she had been alive. There are times when I would be better speaking to the kitchen table. It wouldn't ask damn silly questions."

He rose smartly, put on his raincoat and went out. Not in a huff, as his wife assumed, but to pursue a thought her question had suggested to him.

When he entered one of the village houses, a little later, he was met by Alice Ann, one of his pupils. She was perturbed to see him. It was unusual for the Schoolmaster to go visiting in the village at all, especially at an early hour on a Saturday morning. His greeting set her mind at rest. "Is Easter up yet?"

Although he was hale and hearty, despite his nearly ninety years, and everyone in the house deferred to him, her grandfather, known invariably as Easter, was not involved in matters of family discipline. If the Schoolmaster had come to complain about something she had done – and she could think of nothing – he would have asked for her father, or more likely, her mother.

Reassured, Alice Ann responded brightly, "He's gone for a walk across the machair. Will I take you to him? I know exactly where he'll be."

"Where's that?" asked the Schoolmaster, with an attempt at affability as he motioned to Alice Ann to lead the way.

"Sitting on the hillock where he used to sit as a boy to watch the cattle," she said. "He told me once that they had no fences when he was a boy. I don't think they knew about wire netting and anyway they had no wood to make fencing posts. The only wood they had was what was washed up on the beach in a storm, and you know yourself that's not much. So the boys used to take turns to watch the cattle on the machair and keep them out of the corn."

She broke off suddenly, realising that she might be standing into danger. The Schoolmaster sensed what the story was leading to and put it to her squarely. "So he played truant from school! That's why his mind is stuck in the past, when educated people are thinking of the present and the future."

For the Schoolmaster the past was a great blunder, which he and those who thought like him were born to redeem. Alice Ann, however, missed the import of his comment and continued innocently, "I could listen to him for hours. He has wonderful stories about kings and queens and ghosts and fairies, and strange monsters that lived in the lochs, and seal women singing on the rocks. He can even sing some of the songs. And sometimes he'll tell me how he used to go poaching as a lad, and once the gamekeeper nearly caught him, but he jumped into the river and swam right out to sea, and came ashore in another place where they never thought of looking for him."

"I haven't time for that sort of nonsense, and neither should you!" said the Schoolmaster sharply. "I'll be interested to see whether he can answer the questions I'm going to put to him now. If he can, it will be the first time his obsession with the past has ever been of practical use."

"What are you going to ask him?" asked Alice Ann.

"Never you mind!" said the Schoolmaster. Then, to soften the rebuke he added, "Did he ever tell you about Easter Island?"

"Where's that?"

"You don't even know why your grandfather got his nickname?"

"Why did he?"

"Because he spent many years working on Easter Island. Here's a man who has travelled the world, and seen the evils of colonial exploitation, but he has nothing better to do with his time than sit on a hillock stuffing his grand-daughter with nonsense about fairies."

"Are fairies wicked?" asked Alice Ann.

"No, but the fools who talk about them are."

"Still," added the Schoolmaster reflectively, "one can sometimes find little bits of history mixed up with the rubbish."

By this time they had reached the hillock where Easter was seated, smoking his pipe and gazing into the distant landscape of his own barefooted boyhood.

"You see that headland," he began almost as soon as greetings had been exchanged. Before the Schoolmaster could stop him, he had launched into a long and intricate story about a monster that had come ashore from the sea, different from any of the monsters that were described in other stories. "It wasn't an each uisge, that's for sure," he concluded, as if he had just established a fact of world-shaking importance. Then he added, "An each uisge is what you would call a water horse," which annoyed the Schoolmaster mightily because of the assumption that he recognised the existence of a fabulous beast by any name, and even more because it underlined the fact that the old man was bi-lingual while the Schoolmaster was not. But he held his impatience in check, and listened to several equally improbable tales before he could begin discreetly asking questions. Even then he had to approach his objective cautiously, from the flank.

"I remember Robertson Mor telling me once that his family were the oldest in the township. I think he told me they were in the same croft since the 16th century?"

"I don't know about oldest. And I don't know about centuries. They weren't here any sooner than ourselves." He smiled. "We were like the tinkers. We were pushed this way and that by the Factor. I was born myself before we got the croft we have now. I've heard it said that the Robertson Mors were in the same croft all along. They were good at hanging on to things. So were the Robertson Beags."

As often happens to a man who has been long abroad, he had retained a clearer recollection of the events and stories of his youth than those who had stayed at home, and changed with the changing township. It was different when the pace of change was slower and those who stayed at home handed everything down from generation to generation, quite intact. But, when the township moved into a situation where every vestige of the old way of life was being deliberately jettisoned, so that the young folk could take on board their discos and their TV, men like Easter, who had left home early, retained more of what they knew in their youth than those who had been at home all the time and were dragged into a new and foreign world by their own children.

At first the other villagers thought Easter an eccentric, and they still found him a bore, but, when he was discovered by the School of Scottish Studies as a remarkable repository of legends, proverbs and songs, they were pleased that someone from the village was sought out by professors and researchers, and made a boast of him. All of them, that is, except the Schoolmaster. He was envious that an unlettered villager, whom he despised, should be so regarded, when no one bothered to call at the schoolhouse to hear his own profound and, as he thought, original, views about the political structure of the country and how it should be reformed. He was more than a little resentful that he had to resort to Easter for information, but consoled himself with the thought that he had now got the answer he had hoped for, and could put it to good use.

"You are sure the Robertson Mors had the same croft two hundred years ago as they have today?" he asked, carefully checking over the essential facts.

"I was not there myself to see it," said Easter, "but that is what I have always heard."

"And the same peat ground?"

"There was a row about that once," said Easter. "I had forgotten all about it until you asked me just now. The Factor came to fix the boundaries. When I was a boy. I was there and saw it all. He put a big white stone in the ground at each corner of the lot. We were all there watching, as boys will be, and the Factor spoke to us. A wee runt of a man with a pipe as big as himself. Puff! Puff! Puff! You could see his self-importance in the way he blew the smoke. And the crofters all licking over him like a cat with a kitten. They had to, you know. He was a man of great power."

Easter's comments on the Factor were music in the Schoolmaster's ear. At least they would have been, if he had made them himself, but there is nothing more irritating than to hear a man you despise singing your song, as if he had a right to share your insight. They troubled him too at a deeper level because they came welling up from the past in the talk of a man he regarded as intellectually petrified, raising the question whether his own views on landlordism were really mint fresh, as he liked to think, or just the echo of an echo repeated endlessly throughout the ages. Again he mastered his irritation, with a struggle, and continued his questioning.

"I played him like a ruddy salmon," he told his wife that night. "A great sulky brute, lying at the bottom of a deep dark pool. But I got him to the bank eventually."

With much circumnavigation of the point the Schoolmaster was interested in, Easter had described how the Factor gathered the lads around him with a smile and asked them to remember the planting of the big white stones and what they meant.

"If there's another dispute when you are old men, you can settle it among yourselves without bothering me!"

"And then," said Easter, "he added that we were lucky not to get a thrashing. We all backed away. We knew the Factor could do almost anything, even if the crofters had stood up to him and his kind until they got security of tenure from the Parliament. We didn't want a thrashing. That's for sure. Then he laughed and told us we were quite safe, but in the old days they always thrashed the boys at the spot they put the markers down, so that they would never forget it. Think of that now! They gave them a thrashing and they never forgot it."

"So the peat bank Robertson Mor is using is within the boundaries of the land the family had as far back as you can go?" said the Schoolmaster.

Easter did not reply. He was off on another story. But his silence on the point was good enough. The Schoolmaster broke off the conversation abruptly, almost rudely, and hurried back to the village, to spread the news that the man found in the bog had been murdered by one of Robertson Mor's ancestors.

"It's funny the way it persists in the blood!" he added, sotto voce at the end of each recital. "The chances are that he was a wealthy traveller killed for his money. Robertson Mor wouldn't kill a fly. He hasn't the guts for that. But you don't buy a Mercedes unless you've squeezed someone pretty hard."

By nightfall the whole village believed that an ancestor of Robertson Mor had murdered a pedlar, and hidden the money in the bog. Robertson Mor had stumbled on the treasure, but the pedlar had come back to haunt him.

"I don't believe in ghosts," said the Schoolmaster. "and anyway this body is not a ghost. But if Robertson Mor, or any of his kind is haunted, I'm all for it. It makes me almost believe in the again bite of inwit."

The villagers looked at him uncomprehendingly, but the Schoolmaster was pleased to be able to demonstrate that he had a passing acquaintance with Old English, even if he did not know Modern Gaelic.

The next evening he was furious when the door opened and Easter walked in, without knocking, and took a comfortable seat by the fire, with his bonnet still on his head.

"You should knock the door before you enter a private house," said the Schoolmaster curtly. His wife frowned at him. She knew Easter meant no harm. He had merely followed the custom of the village, in walking freely into a neighbour's house. She shared her husband's desire for privacy, but, at the same time, she did not want to be lampooned in the village for pride.

"Yes," said Easter slowly, lighting his pipe and filling the room with the heavy smoke of thick black twist, "I used to knock in Easter Island, but I was a stranger there!"

The rebuke infuriated the Schoolmaster still further, because it reminded him of the parochial life he had led, but his wife's look checked him, and he remained gloomily silent during a dreary hour while Easter discoursed about the weather, his experiences on Easter Island, and his journeys back and fore.

"Is there something you particularly want to say to me?" asked the Schoolmaster at last. He didn't try to hide his impatience.

"I thought you were interested in Robertson Mor's croft!" said Easter with surprise, as if he had been speaking about the croft all evening, whereas he had not even got round to mentioning it.

The Schoolmaster realised then that Easter had remembered some additional information about the croft, which might or might not be relevant. He could only discover which, if he contained himself until Easter decided that the time was ripe for him to come to the point.

"There was once a man from the village who went to college," he said at last. "That was in the days before it was easy for any fool to go. It made a great sensation. It had never been heard of before. But he had two brothers. When he came back from college he tricked them out of their inheritance because he could write and they could not. One of them killed him, but we never knew which."

"This happened in your own lifetime?" asked the Schoolmaster, incredulously, fastening on the "we".

"I told you it didn't!" replied Easter, surprised at the Schoolmaster's stupidity. He had not noticed the significance of "we", which he used merely to identify himself with the continuing history of the village.

Seeing that the Schoolmaster was still puzzled he began to count on his fingers. "It was in the time of my seven grandfathers back!"

"Where did you get the story?" asked the Schoolmaster, afraid the old man had made it up.

"It has always been in our family," said Easter. "I heard it first when I was a little boy, but I forgot it until I began to think over the questions you put to me yesterday. I could tell you exactly where I was standing when my mother told it to me first."

"Don't jump to conclusions!" Margaret whispered to her husband. "His people were never very reliable."

"God, woman!" said the Schoolmaster, impatiently. "He's telling the truth. The murdered man was a scholar. The paper says he was carrying a satchel with writing implements in it."

"Many another man had pen and ink!" retorted Margaret.

"Not at that time, stupid!" said the Schoolmaster. "The dates fit, if we average Easter's generations at thirty years each, or so."

"What else do you know?" he asked.

Easter paused and blew great clouds of smoke across the room. It was almost as if he was enjoying the Schoolmaster's impatience as much as he was enjoying the telling of his story.

At last he put the pipe in his pocket, and, looking straight at the Schoolmaster, said, "One of the brothers was Robertson Mor and the other was Robertson Beag, but we don't know which killed the scholar."

"Rubbish!" said Margaret. "You said yourself it happened hundreds of years ago."

"He means that Robertson Mor and Robertson Beag are descended from the two brothers," said the Schoolmaster peevishly. "I knew they were related if you could go far enough back, and it always puzzled me that, living so close together, they were not related more recently. One would have expected these two families to inter-marry over the generations. Perhaps we know now why they didn't."

"Indeed we do not!" said Margaret with an emphasis which startled her husband. He was not used to being contradicted. "This is ancient history. If it is history at all. The sooner you forget it the better. I have often heard you say yourself it would be a God's blessing if we could forget the past and get on with what's in front of us. Although what you have to do with God I wouldn't know. When you go to church you have a book on politics hidden inside a black cover you took from an old Bible!"

Easter raised his eyebrows, but said nothing. Although he was interested mainly in the past, he was not deaf to current gossip. This was a juicy titbit for the village.

The Schoolmaster disregarded his wife's outburst. He had heard it all before, although this was the first time she had mentioned his church-going habits before a third party.

"I've now got them in my power! Both of them!" he gloated. "The murdered man was found on Robertson Mor's land, but who put him there? If you murder your brother do you bury him in your own garden or in someone else's, if you have the chance?"

"You can't send a man to gaol for what his ancestors did seven generations back!" said Margaret.

"Whose speaking of gaol?" demanded the Schoolmaster. "I'm speaking about power. Political power. These two men have ruled the village ever since I came here. Everyone thinks of them as rivals. Enemies. They're not. They belong to the same class. They stick together. At least they have until now. I'll set them at each other's throats. Intelligence will take over from greed in Kilmanoevaig."

He turned to Easter. "You just go through the village now telling them all you've told me. They'll be very interested."

"A grain of mustard seed!" he said to Margaret as Easter left.

The Biblical analogy was probably planted in his mind by her own comment on his church-going habits, but he had already forgotten that indiscretion, in his anxiety to see the Robertsons brought low.

There was generally a silent groan when Easter dropped into a neighbour's house, he was such an unmitigated bore. But that evening he was welcome everywhere. He never got round to talking about the Robertsons. His story of the Schoolmaster going to church with 'Das Kapital', hidden in the cover torn from a Bible, was the best bone the villagers had to gnaw for a long time. They scraped it clean. They buried it. They dug it up again. They took it into corners to gloat. They quarrelled for possession of it. But, above all, they laughed. And those who laughed loudest were those who shared the Schoolmaster's ambivalent attitude to church, attending regularly for appearance sake, but carrying with them extraneous interests of their own, concealed about the person or the mind. Their laughter was partly camouflage, partly delight at having found an ally, partly pleasure at seeing the mighty Schoolmaster brought low. He was no better than themselves.

The Kirk Session took the matter seriously. They would have liked to show their displeasure by refusing him admittance. He took that weapon from them by not going. He knew that, if he did, half the congregation would scramble to sit near him to see what particular contraband he was carrying that day, while the other half would avoid him like a leper.

He abused his wife in private for her indiscretion. It irked him that he could not blame her in public as well. He wanted to dissociate himself in the eyes of the village from her stupidity. But how could he? Except, perhaps, by laughing at himself, and he had not reached that stage of maturity. Nor did he aspire to it, because he did not see it as a goal.

He used the incident, however, to bar the door of the schoolhouse against Easter, which scandalised the village even more than his behaviour in church. For the first time they saw him as a social, as well as an intellectual, snob.

Although the scandal about the Schoolmaster diverted the attention of the village from the mystery of the body in the bog and Robertson Mor's sudden access of prosperity, the poison he sought to spread did its work effectively in another way.

At first the two Robertsons joked about the old tale which now linked their families.

"Let's see your hands!" said Robertson Beag to his neighbour the first time they met. There was no need to explain that he was looking for traces of blood.

"Let's see your own!" replied Robertson Mor with a laugh.

"We'll walk through the village together. That'll make the buggers talk. They expect us to be at each other's throats." said Robertson Beag.

Robertson Mor accepted the invitation with a laugh and took his rival's arm. It was most unusual for two grown men to be seen walking through the village with no obvious destination or purpose, and almost beyond belief that they should walk with arms linked like a couple of girls. They were watched from every window as they passed, and there was great speculation about the reason for their strange behaviour.

"It must be something terribly important if they don't want their wives to hear it," was the general interpretation. And then the guessing game began.

"They're going into partnership!"

"Robertson Mor is taking him over!"

"Robertson Mor is going bankrupt. That's why he bought the car."

"They're forming a ring to screw the knitters down!"

"They're swopping wives like the toffs in the News of the World!"

"Robertson Beag has cancer. He's asking Robertson Mor to look after his affairs."

It would be wrong to say that the curiosity of the villagers filtered back to the two wives. It surrounded them like a magnetic field. They felt it even when they didn't hear it, gaining urgency, momentum and pitch with every repetition and embellishment.

When quizzed about their walk, in the privacy of their homes, the two men laughed. They described the incident exactly as it happened. Neither of the wives was satisfied. It was too childish. Besides, one of the wives was envious of her neighbour's wealth. The other was irked by the restraint she was under in displaying her own.

"There is a connection between Robertson Mor's money and that body in the bog," persisted Janet. "If not, why aren't we as rich?"

"Now they think you found a fortune in the bog why can't we splash it around?" asked Mary.

The two men continued in the cautious line they had adopted from the start. They knew that they needed each other. But the pressures were too insistent.

"For God's sake, tell me where your money came from?" said Robertson Beag at last. "I don't give a damn myself but I want to set Janet's mind at rest. She thinks I'm a fool when I can't do as well myself."

"Tell her it's a disaster that might fall on you just as it fell on me," said Robertson Mor.

"The pools!" said Robertson Beag.

"I didn't say so," said Robertson Mor. Then, after a pause he added, "There's only one way to sort this out. I have more money than I ever dreamt of, but I can't spend it here. I'll retire to the south of England and enjoy my freedom. You'll have a monopoly of the local wool. A monopoly of the Kilmanoevaig knitters. A monopoly of the name. You can't go wrong. When you've made your pile you can come south and join me."

"Why stop at the south of England. Let's be tax exiles," said Robertson Beag, warming to the prospect.

"Or gossip exiles, to escape their bleeding tongues," said Robertson Mor.

And that is what happened. More or less!

The Robertson Mors retired to the Channel Islands, where they tried to pretend they were happy, but died of boredom. The Robertson Beags had a few years of growing affluence, but were bankrupt within five years.

Without the spur of competition, Robertson Beag became lazy and greedy. The buyers got tired of his unimaginative patterns and soaring prices. The crofters found other markets for their high grade wool. The knitters, who had accepted low wages for years under the illusion that they were cleverly playing one employer off against the other, now made excessive demands, compounding their employer's greed.

"It's a dying village," said the Schoolmaster disconsolately, as he looked at the school roll, dwindling from year to year, as families left in search of greener pastures. When it was finally downgraded to one-teacher status, his loneliness was intense. He had slammed the door in the faces of his neighbours, and he no longer had a captive assistant whom he could lecture on politics and educational theory. He couldn't even sneak to church, as in the past, to sugar his sterile beliefs with a little surreptitious religion. Although he had not realised it at the time, that was what he had really been doing.

As for the body of the student mummified by the peat – it is now one of the most popular exhibits in a city museum. Colour apart, the clothing has been preserved exactly as it was. The features too are perfectly composed. The victim was struck down from behind and didn't have time even to look surprised. He gazes quizzically at the crowd, almost as if he were returning their stare: sharp, intelligent, amused.

"You would think he was still alive," is a frequent comment.

And perhaps he is: in the lingering myths which shape men's lives, and sometimes tear communities apart.

Mairead's Window

EVERY NIGHT, BEFORE SHE WENT TO BED, Mairead walked into the little parlour I rented from her, at the end of the house, and stood at the window, audibly counting the lights in the village. I have heard her on many occasions. Indeed, if I was reading, she would switch off my table lamp abruptly, as if she were unaware of my presence, and draw aside the curtains, peering out from the darkened room, while she made her count. On the way out, she would suddenly remember I was there, switch on the lamp again, and apologise.

"You must excuse a foolish old woman," was all she ever said before slipping quietly off to bed and her dreams.

I often stood at the window myself, in the darkness, sometimes for hours at a stretch, for a very different reason, and looking almost at a different scene.

Mairead's house was a little apart from the others, on one of the horns of the bay. It faced in the same general direction but, standing on a little headland, it was a step in front of them, so to speak, and had the sea on three sides instead of just along the frontage. It also commanded a view along the sound between the mountains, so that one could see, as through a telescope, the storm clouds marshalling on the peaks of the neighbouring island, hours before they descended in fury on ourselves. Even more importantly, from Mairead's point of view, and sometimes from my own, the fact that the house was stepped forward from the others meant that, from the end window of the parlour, one had an uninterrupted view of every other house front. Her own was private, like herself, visible only for fleeting moments from passing ships at sea, and always heavily curtained, against even the remote contingency of peering.

It took me years of regular visits, as a summer boarder, to penetrate her reserve and tap the hidden springs. The nightly ritual at the parlour window gave me the occasion and the clue. When I stood at the parlour window, my interest was not in the lights which Mairead counted, square or oblong, static and precise, but in the soundless madrigal played out by the reflections in the bay below. It was a dance, undoubtedly, but I could not think of it as ballet. The movements were too abrupt. They were severed completely when a ripple crossed them, as movements in a ballet can never be. The elements which made up the harmony were discrete, discontinuous, disembodied – notes of light, entirely separate from each other and the instrument from which they came. Although I am a painter by profession, the only moment at which I thought of the nightly pageant as visual, rather than audible, was when the last light in the village was switched off and the bay went black, with the sudden predestined finality of the curtain at the end of a performance. There was no applause, but I could almost fancy that there was, because I became conscious then of the rhythmic wash of the waves on the shingle beach, which I did not notice as I "listened" to the lights. Invariably, when the lights went out and the sounds came up, I thought of Tennyson and his "Break! Break! Break!" At that point a sombre sequence of ideas flowed through my mind, wave after wave.

The dance of light, so swift, so utterly random, so tantalising! I always longed to get my brushes out to capture it on canvas. But how do you paint a Will O' the Wisp? A three dimensional Picasso of rippling fire? A dance of demented hobgoblins, who change their shape more quickly than you can perceive it? And yet this evanescent, unrepeatable, sequence of flickering lights is precise and predetermined.

The basic shapes are simple, rigid, geometrical; straight-edged distortions of the windows, according to unvarying laws of optics, by which the proportions are altered and even the category of figure, but not the kind. These are then broken by the waves, equally regular, equally determinate, moving in a curved diagonal sweep against the plane of light, disturbed sometimes by secondary waves set up by sudden flurries of wind, or the wash of a boat, passing in the dark, just beyond the headland, but still obeying well established rules, even in the utmost confusion.

"Here am I, an artist," I would say, "and I cannot paint what I see. I cannot even see what I see. It changes too quickly for me to grasp. And yet, if I were God, I could paint it before it happened. It is fore-ordained in the static lights and the rhythm of the water."

The thought of my own inadequacy before God was not the trough of my dismay. I was not in competition with the Almighty. There was something reassuring, or even exalting, in the contrast. Until the thought occurred to me that, if I were not God but only a supreme mathematician, I could still predict the picture that I cannot paint. And then there always came the final blow. The last exterminating thought. No such mathematician will ever exist. But we do not need him. A dull technician, mole blind to the wonder of the universe, could one day programme a computer to tabulate my moving lights and paint them for me, before they happened.

At that point I would crawl to bed, not humbled but humiliated. Thinking of myself as a silly child trying to build a palace with his little bricks, while navvies and plumbers across the street were building the real thing, with no sense of wonder, no pride in their achievement; no higher ambition than to get to pay day as quickly as they could, and forget it all in the fug and clamour of a crowded bar.

I generally consoled myself with the thought that, at least, I had the sensitivity to know my predicament, unlike old Mairead, shuffling through life by rote, from sink to pan, from pan to table, from table to bed, pausing only for the nightly head count of the summer visitors, who occupied the village from June to August, but who, by mid-September, or the beginning of October at the latest, would pack their bags, load up their motor cars, and return to the city, leaving her alone, a black ghost, in a darkened landscape, with no one to speak to, not even anyone to count.

I asked her once, "What do you do in winter when the lights have all gone out? Do you still come to the window before you go to bed?"

"It is easier in a way, when there are no lights," she replied. "They come between me and what I want to see."

She was gone, silently, before I could follow it up, but, having broken the ice, and mentioned what previously had seemed too private a matter to be discussed, I came back to it, cautiously, a few days later.

When I questioned her, she replied, unexpectedly, "Have you ever been to a picture house?" as if it were unlikely, almost inconceivable, like asking me had I ever picnicked on the top of Everest. A visit to the picture house must have been a rare, perhaps a unique, event, in her quiet life.

"Many times," I replied. "Why do you ask?"

"They're like the picture house," she replied. "The lights! They're not real people at all behind the windows. None of them were born. None of them die. None of them get married. They don't even quarrel. Sometimes one or two of them get drunk. It's as near as they get to being flesh and blood."

"I can assure you they have all been born somewhere," I said with a laugh. "And most of them have been married somewhere, although I cannot vouch for that. One thing sure is they will all die sometime, somewhere."

"Somewhere!" she echoed. "That's just it. It's not here. It's not anywhere together. They don't belong to each other at all.

"If I go down to the hen run with a handful of grain, the hens will come squawking around me from all sides, rolling about on their great stiff legs as if they would fall over in their hurry. The cockerel will be there, as proud as Lucifer, lording it over them, and the chickens at their feet. In the morning there may be eggs, and now and then a broody hen. I know them all by name. Sweetie Box. Red Feather. Tombola. Why did I call her that? It's a word I heard on the wireless. I don't know what it means, but somehow it suits her. She's a great boss. There must be a bit of the cockerel in her. That's it. That's why I called her Tombola, although I didn't know it. She's a tomboy.

"Now, if I go out with grain to the grass in front of the house, it's the seagulls that'll come, and the black backs, dropping out of the sky, every man for himself, and off again as soon as they're fed. The hens belong together, and they belong to me, and they're some use in the world. I used to belong to my neighbours, and I helped them. Even when I hated them. But it's not like that any more. No one belongs to anyone in this place now. We need hens, but what's the sense in seagulls?"

"The Good Lord made the seagulls too," I replied, using the sort of language she might have used herself. "He must have had a reason for it."

"Maybe he had," she said with a chuckle, "but I can't see it! Any more than I can see the sense of them!" She waved her arm comprehensively in the direction of the other houses. "They're not real at all! They're make believe. It's not that I amn't friendly with them. And they're very nice. Some of them will even pass the time of day. Sometimes they come to see will I sell them eggs or milk. One or two of them have even brought me little gifts, when I gave them something and wouldn't take payment. And I like to see the children enjoying themselves. The children are all right. It's the others that trouble me. How do you know a man or a woman if you have never seen them ill, or sorrowing? Or rejoicing over something real like the father when his prodigal son came home? That's why I count the lights every night. Waiting for them to go, so that the village will come alive again."

"Alive!" I said incredulously, thinking of her long winter hibernation, in a boarded up village. Alone!

"Alive!" she repeated. "The ghosts of the dead are more alive than the ghosts of the living. At least they were real once."

She sat down suddenly, as if to begin a conversation, something she had never done before. Then, just as suddenly, she got up again, took me by the arm and led me to the window.

"You see the light that isn't there at the end of the village?" she said.

"You mean there's a house that's dark, beyond the last that's lit?" I asked.

"Yes," she replied.

"I'll take your word for it, but I cannot see it."

"When you know what should be there as well as I do, you can see what isn't, as clearly as what is," she said. "The Robinsons have gone away. That's why that light's out. And fair wind after them! I have never spoken to them although they've been coming here for every day of ten years. When I meet them, she gives me a look that makes me feel like dirt under her feet. It's a sad end for the Unicorn's house. In spite of the big bay windows, and the roses they put in the garden. It was better for me when the Unicorn had sheep in it."

"Why did they call him the Unicorn?" I asked to keep her talking.

"It's well seen he was before your time," she replied. "He had a big wart on the point of his nose, standing straight up, with black hairs growing out of it, and a big red birth mark that covered half his face. He was the ugliest man I ever knew, and the jolliest. They say he had a great way with the ladies. At least he said it himself. When he was a little drunk he used to boast that half the children in the village were his. But I don't believe it. There wasn't another wart in the village, or an ugly face worth mentioning, but his own. If he fathered all these bairns, he must have left his mark on some of them. But he was good fun at a ceilidh, making the women blush, accusing them of things

I couldn't tell you. Most times the husbands joined in the fun, but sometimes they took it seriously, and heaven knows what happened when they went back to their own homes. But he never made fun of his next door neighbour. You couldn't make fun with the Pope. That's why he got the name. You never saw anyone stiffer. And you couldn't find a fault in him. If he spilt a pail of milk on the floor, he would swear blind the milk was still in the pail, supposing the cat was there at his feet licking it up.

"He had eight of a family. The two girls were as stubborn as himself. Big and noisy. I wouldn't like to be the man that married either of them. But the six boys were like roe deer, staring there at you with mournful eyes, but, if you as much as moved a muscle, they were away up the hill, running for their lives. He couldn't have taken the spirit out of them better, supposing he had put them through the mangle."

At this point she lowered her voice confidentially, although there was no one in the house but the two of us.

"They say his family was bigger even than it looked. I wouldn't be surprised if he was the father of the children the Unicorn boasted about. People are funny like that; always pretending to be something other than they are. In a small place like this, you see them naked and you see them dressed. I don't mean with their clothes off. But you see the real man behind the man he's pretending to be. In glimpses anyway. Even in Drumguish, where we were all living in each others' kitchens until the strangers took it over, you could never be sure. Even if someone was caught redhanded, it would be a different story by the time it got half way down the street, maybe with different people in it. That's what made everyone so real for me. I never knew the truth about them, but I was always trying to find out. The people who are here today are of no more interest than the gatepost. When you've seen them once, you know all that you'll ever find out. But the old folk were like the mountains. Always there, but always changing. You could never be sure how much was them and how much was the weather, when you looked out and saw them. And even if you climbed them to the top, or walked all over them, there were deep gulleys that you never got into, and little flowers between the rocks to surprise you.

"Night after night I'm still going through the village, looking at all the children that used to be there, and saying to myself, now, was he his father's or was he the Pope's? Or maybe the Unicorn was telling the truth even if he didn't pass his warts to him! They're still there because I still want to know about them. And every night I come to the same conclusion. Most of them were their fathers' children just as surely as their mothers', but, if there wasn't the doubt, I would have forgotten them long ago."

"You never married?" I asked, checking myself, just in time, from saying, "You didn't have a family yourself?" I had always called her Miss Maclean, and, in that context, my question would have been too pointed, although I did not really know whether she was Mrs or Miss.

She smiled, as if she had seen me avoiding the trap. "I did and I didn't," she replied. "See! That's the house. Where the light has just gone out. And the one beside it with the two lights still burning. They're always the last to go to bed."

"What do you mean 'That's the house'?" I asked. "You've mentioned two."

"He went to the university," she said, ignoring my question. "He became a minister. A famous minister. I still see his name in the papers, now and then, although he's old like myself."

"Is that why you didn't marry?" I asked, as gently as I could. "He moved on in the world and forgot the little village he came from."

"What do you mean by marry?" she asked. "I never stood beside him in church to get a ring on my finger, but we were married if ever two people were. And we are married still. I never got him out of my bones, and he has not forgotten me, even if his own children are now university professors and members of Parliament."

"How do you know he still remembers you?" I asked.

"Because he never comes to see me," she replied. "He comes often to the north to preach, and sometimes on holiday. If I was just an old woman, a friend of his childhood living by myself in an empty village, he would be here to see me whenever he could. He's kindness itself to the old people in all the villages round about. He is keeping away from me because he is desperate to come. Besides he's afraid of what he'll find. There are ghosts in this house too, and he's afraid to meet them."

"You think he may see you with his memory, rather than his eye," I said. I had often appraised with an artist's intensity the fine bone structure, beneath the brown and leathery skin. I had even toyed with the idea of getting her to sit as model for a series of portraits in which I would try to peel off the accumulation of the years, and trace the gracious stages in the transformation of the young Madonna, whose beauty inspired lust and malice as well as love, into the saintly Mother of God, sorrowing serenely at the foot of the Cross.

"It's not his memory of me he's afraid of. It's his memory of himself."

I wanted to question her further, but felt her recollection was too sensitive for probing, and I sat in absolute stillness, listening to my own held breath, hoping that out of the long continued silence she would be constrained to speak again.

"There was a dance that night," she said at last. "Just where we are sitting. My father's barn was here then, before he built the new house. This room is still the barn to me. I smell the meal whenever I come into it, and the sweat of the dancers. Before I reach the window I can see them swirling round, and me in the middle, laughing and hooching, and burning with pleasure, like a peat when you lift it with the tongs and blow on it with your mouth. By the time I reach the window, it's silent again, and they're all back in their own homes, and I can see them as they were, from the cradle almost to the grave. Every one of them a mystery to me still, although I knew them all their lives.

"John and I were pledged to each other then. He was at the college, and I was going into service to be near him in the city. I had written secretly for the job. I knew my father would not want me to leave home while my mother was unwell, but I was thinking of myself.

"His neighbour was at the dance as well. Big Dan Finlayson. Like a pine tree, with great spreading arms, and a dark head towering over everyone else in the village. He was a seaman and he hadn't been at home for three or four years. I was just a child when he left, but, as soon as he came into the barn, his face lit up and he elbowed his way through the crowd to get to me. Dance after dance after dance, he kept me to himself. A grown man who had seen the world. He had no eyes for anyone in the village but me. Whenever John came near, he brushed him aside like a fly. At last he said to him, 'If you want to get her back, step outside and take her from me.'

"Without a word, John walked out of the barn. If his walk had been different, Dan would have followed him, and he might have been killed there in the darkness, because no one could have stood up to that giant. But that was not the way he walked, and I joined with the others in a great mocking laugh as he left.

"Dan called to the piper. There was no wall then where the bookcase is. The piper was right at the other end of the barn, where we built the kitchen. I sometimes see him standing beside me when I cook your supper. 'Give us a reel!' said Dan. He took me by the hand, as the piper began to fill his bag, and I stood with him in the middle of the floor feeling prouder than I had ever been.

"And then I saw that no one else was joining in the dance. The lads were all at one end of the barn, and the girls at the other, staring at the two of us. Let them stare! I danced as if my life depended on it. But, when the piper stopped and we were there alone in the middle of the floor, I wondered why the whole world was not sharing my happiness. I looked at their faces. It was then it came to me that I was the coward, not John. I had let myself be turned aside from the thing I most wanted in life by flattery and fear.

"I ran from the hall before he could stop me and raced along the beach. It was more direct than the road. All the houses in the village were dark except one. I knew John had reached home. But if I could get there before the light went out, I would be safe. Many a time before that I had tapped on his window, when he was studying and I wanted to see him.

"The light was still burning when I came to the burn. It was swollen by the rain and I could not wade it, even where it spread out across the beach. I ran up towards the road, and over the bridge, but, when the house was in view again, the window was dark.

"I turned back home, but I could hear the voices of groups coming from the dance. It must have stopped whenever I left. I knew they were all talking about me. Earlier I had welcomed their eyes and their envy. Now I was afraid of their tongues. Not their malice but their knowledge. They knew I had made a fool of myself. They knew before I did. And now that I knew, it was bitter to hear their laughter.

"I left the road and came home through the moor. I was scared of the bogs and the sheep wandering in the dark. The tups were on the hill and I thought they might attack me. I hadn't time to think of ghosts. I was more frightened of the people on the road."

She paused for a moment.

"It's funny! I was frightened of the kind of ghost we had then, although they weren't there at all, but now it's the ghosts, the real ghosts, that keep me company. I think I could take you every step of the way I took that night, along the shore, and through the moor. I could tell you every voice I heard, and where I heard it, and what I thought it was saying.

"But more than anything else, I was scared of Dan. I knew well enough what he wanted from me. And I knew he would not scruple, even if he had to use his strength. That was what attracted me, until the staring eyes of the other dancers brought me to my senses. I thought I could hear his feet scrunching on the beach when I ran along it. Then I thought I could hear the rustle of his step in the heather. I never found out whether he followed me or not. I got home wet and muddy, and sneaked away to bed.

"I never saw John again. He went off the next day, although the college did not open for weeks. He never wrote, and I could not write him. It still stands between us. If he had blamed me and I had blamed him, we would have quarrelled and made it up. But we blamed ourselves. There was nothing to quarrel about and nothing to forgive."

"Don't think I didn't have a happy life," she continued, after another pause. "I was very contented here as long as there was a village to be contented in. Even when my son left home, I always had his next home-coming to look forward to. I still had pleasures in front of me then. Now they are all behind me. Except the one."

In other circumstances I would have liked to probe more deeply into her serene acceptance of death as another homecoming. Instead I murmured gently, "Tell me about your son."

She smiled. "You're wondering who the father was? That was the one child in the village I never had any doubt about, although no one else was sure but me."

After a pause she added, "That's another reason why his father never comes to see me. He doesn't know which to fear most, that the boy was his, or that he wasn't."

It was then, for the first time, I realised the significance of one particular photograph, among the scores with which the room was cluttered. Many of them were unframed, faded, creased or stained, as if they had travelled far, which most of them obviously had, in time, if not in space. There were so many of them I had come to the conclusion that she made a practice of gathering the family portraits from each house in the village as it fell empty, before it was taken over by strangers. She was gathering all the memorials of the vanished community to herself, as the last custodian.

The photograph which stood out from the others had a wooden frame, obviously of eastern origin. Not Chinese or Indian, I thought, but possibly from Java. It was of a young ship's captain who bore a strong resemblance to his mother, although her wrinkles somewhat blurred the likeness. In the past I had taken it as evidence of the persistence of a family resemblance, in a collateral line, drawing genes from a common source.

As if taking up my unspoken thought, she crossed the room and took the photograph in her hand. "He didn't let his father down, although neither knew who the other was," she said. "They told me he was the youngest captain in the merchant navy when his ship was sunk, and they gave him a medal after he was dead."

She put her hand inside her blouse, and brought the medal out. She had worn it all these years, as she might have worn a crucifix, had that been the tradition of her church.

"It must have been a struggle bringing up a child without a father," I said, more to fill a pause than fish for information.

"That's the funny bit," she said with a laugh. "The neighbours were very good to me, as you would expect. Even the Pope. Once the elders and the minister were done with me! But the person who helped me most was big Dan Finlayson."

For a moment I wondered if I had misunderstood what she had said to me earlier about the father, and she caught the puzzlement in my face.

"No! No! No!" she said. "Dan had nothing to do with the boy. But his pride was touched when I turned him down. He used to send me money from places I never heard of, to make the village think he was more of a man than he really was. I have the envelopes yet. He was not a man to be married to, but he had a kind heart, and, if he ever had a shilling, he spent it on his friends."

She rose abruptly. "I don't know why I'm telling you all this nonsense. It doesn't matter now to anyone but me."

Before I could comment, she had left the room.

When she died, not long after, I was surprised to learn that she had left a will, naming me as executor and sole legatee. The will was written after our long talk together, and I felt that I was the inheritor of her personal history rather than her estate, which consisted of nothing but the tumbledown cottage on the shore.

It must have cost her a considerable effort, to say nothing of money, to make the will. People in her situation are not ready to make wills even when they have a lawyer close at hand. For her, the nearest lawyer was miles away, and there was no public transport. The new villagers had no need of buses during their summer sojourn. They had their cars and caravans and boats, and the sole survivor of the real village was too insignificant to count statistically. People no longer exist, except as crowds.

I still go to the window every night before retiring, as Mairead did for so many years, and as I did myself so frequently while she was still alive. Her ghosts are all gone. Or rather they live with me, tenuously. The ghosts of ghosts. A fading echo of what once was life.

Since her death, and partly because of it, my painting has become even more obscure and difficult. In the past I attempted the impossible task of capturing the music of the moving lights on inert canvas. Now I am trying to capture something even more elusive; the spirit of a village which has died. A village of which nothing remains but an empty shell, in and around which a new summer village has arisen. Phoenix like but utterly different. How does one represent the relationship - and the differences – between the two?

Sometimes I paint from the vast collection of fading photographs I have inherited, many of them taken thousands of miles from the old village, but still part of it. Oddly enough there is a vogue for my phantasmagoria, as I call them – a broth of sepia faces, floating round the canvas, as I explore the relationship between youth and age, generation and generation, resemblances and mutations, as they persist or arise. But that is not at all what I am seeking. I am trying to illuminate, for myself, if for no one else, the insubstantial but perdurable ties which wove them into a living community, in a way we have lost the secret of.